UNCLE WIGGILY'S TRAVELS

HOWARD R. GARIS

1ST WORLD
LIBRARY
Literary Society

Uncle Wiggily's Travels

Howard R. Garis

© 1st World Library, 2010
PO Box 2211
Fairfield, IA 52556
www.1stworldlibrary.com
Second Edition

LCCN: 2009942650

Softcover ISBN: 978-1-4218-5015-3
Hardcover ISBN: 978-1-4218-5113-6

Purchase *"Uncle Wiggily's Travels"*
as a traditional bound book at:
www.1stWorldLibrary.com/purchase.asp?ISBN=978-1-4218-5015-3

1st World Library is a literary, educational organization
dedicated to:

- Creating a free internet library of downloadable ebooks.

- Hosting writing competitions and offering book
publishing scholarships.

Interested in more 1st World Library books?
contact: literacy@1stworldlibrary.com
Check us out at: www.1stworldlibrary.com

1st World Library Literary Society

Giving Back to the World

"If you want to work on the core problem, it's early school literacy."

- James Barksdale, former CEO of Netscape

"No skill is more crucial to the future of a child, or to a democratic and prosperous society, than literacy."

- Los Angeles Times

Literacy... means far more than learning how to read and write... The aim is to transmit... knowledge and promote social participation."

- UNESCO

"Literacy is not a luxury, it is a right and a responsibility. If our world is to meet the challenges of the twenty-first century we must harness the energy and creativity of all our citizens."

- President Bill Clinton

"Parents should be encouraged to read to their children, and teachers should be equipped with all available techniques for teaching literacy, so the varying needs and capacities of individual kids can be taken into account."

- Hugh Mackay

CONTENTS

STORY I

UNCLE WIGGILY AND THE RED SQUIRREL

You know when Uncle Wiggily Longears, the old rabbit gentleman, started out to look for his fortune, he had to travel many weary miles, and many adventures happened to him. Some of those adventures I have told you in the book just before this one, and now I am going to tell you about his travels when he hoped to find a lot of money, so he would be rich.

One day, as I told you in the last story in the other book, Uncle Wiggily came to a farm, and there he had quite an adventure with a little boy. And this little boy had on red trousers, because, I guess, his blue ones were in the washtub. Anyhow, he and the rabbit gentleman became good friends.

And now I am going to tell you what happened when Uncle Wiggily met the red squirrel.

"Where do you think you will go to look for your fortune to-day, Uncle Wiggily?" asked the little boy with the red trousers the next morning, after the rabbit had stayed all night at the farm house.

"I do not know," said the rabbit gentleman. "Perhaps I had better do some traveling at night. I couldn't find the pot of gold at the end of the rainbow, but perhaps there may be a gold, or silver fortune, at the end of a moon-beam. I think

I'll try."

"Oh, but don't you get sleepy at night?" asked the little boy's mother as she fried an ice cream cone for Uncle Wiggily's breakfast.

"Well, I could sleep in the day time, and then I would stay awake at night," answered the traveling uncle, blinking his ears.

"Oh, but aren't you afraid of the bogeyman at night?" inquired the boy with the red hair - I mean trousers.

"There are no such things as bogeymen," said Uncle Wiggily, "and if there were any, they would not harm you. I am not a bit afraid in the dark, except that I don't like mosquitoes to bite me. I think I'll travel to-morrow night, and look for gold at the end of the moon-beam."

So he started off that day, and he went only a short distance, for he wanted to find a place to sleep in order that he would be wide awake when it got dark.

Well, he found a nice, soft place under a pile of hay, and there he stretched out to slumber as nicely as if he were in his bed at home. He even snored a little bit, I believe, or else it was Bully Frog croaking one of his songs.

The day passed, and the sun went down, and it got all ready to be night, and still Uncle Wiggily slept on soundly. But all of a sudden he heard voices whispering:

"Now you go that way and I'll go this way, and we'll catch that rabbit and put him in a cage and sell him!"

Well, you can just believe that Uncle Wiggily was frightened when he awakened suddenly and saw two bad boys softly creeping up and making ready to catch him.

Howard R. Garis

"Oh, this is no place for me!" the rabbit cried, and he grabbed up his crutch and his valise and hopped away so fast that the boys couldn't catch him, no matter how fast they could run, even bare-footed.

"Let's throw stones at him!" they cried. And they did, but I'm glad to say that none of them hit Uncle Wiggily. Isn't it queer how mean some boys can be? But perhaps they were never told any better, so we'll forgive them this time.

"Well, it is now night," said the rabbit gentleman as he hopped on through the woods, "so I think I will sit under this tree and wait for the moon to come up. And while I'm waiting I'll eat my supper."

So Uncle Wiggily ate his supper, which the kind farmer lady had put up for him, and then he sat and waited for the moon to rise, and pretty soon he heard a funny noise, calling like this:

"Who? Who? Who-tu-tu-tu."

"Oh, you know who I am all right, Mr. Owl," said the rabbit. "You can see very well at night. You can see me."

"My goodness, if it isn't Uncle Wiggily!" cried the owl in surprise. "What are you doing out so late, I'd like to know?"

"Waiting for a moon-beam, so I can see if there is any gold for my fortune at the end of it," was the answer. "Is the moon coming up over the trees, Mr. Owl?"

"Yes, here it comes," said the owl, "and now I must fly off to the dark woods, for I don't like the light," and he fluttered away.

Then the moon came up, all silver and glorious; shining over the tree tops like a shimmering ball, and soon the moon-beams fell to the ground in slanting rays, but they fell so softly, like feathers, that they did not get hurt at all.

"Well, I guess I'll follow that big one," said the old gentleman rabbit, as he picked out a nice, broad, large, shiny moon-beam. "That must have gold at the end, and, if I find it, my fortune is made." So off he started to follow the moon-beam to where it came to an end.

It seemed to go quite a distance through the dark woods, and Uncle Wiggily traveled on for several hours, and he didn't seem to be any nearer the end by that time than he was at first.

"My land, this is a very long beam," he exclaimed. "It is almost big enough to make a church steeple from. But I'll keep on a little longer, for I'm not a bit sleepy yet."

Well, all of a sudden, just as he was turning the corner around a big stone, the rabbit gentleman heard a funny noise.

It wasn't like any one crying, yet it sounded as if some one was in trouble, for the voice said:

"Oh, dear! I'll never get it big enough, I know I can't! I've combed it and brushed it, and done it up in curl papers to make it fluffy, but still it isn't like theirs. What shall I do?"

"Hum, I wonder who that can be?" thought Uncle Wiggily. "Perhaps it is some little lost child; but no children would be out in the woods at night. I'll take a look."

So he hopped softly over, and peered around the edge of the stone, and what do you think he saw?

Why, there was a nice, little, red squirrel-girl, and she had a comb and a brush, and little looking-glass. And the glass was stuck up on a stump where the moon-beam that Uncle Wiggily was following shone on it and reflected back again. And by the light of the moon-beam the red squirrel was combing and brushing out her tail as hard as she could comb

Howard R. Garis

and brush it.

"What are you doing?" asked Uncle Wiggily in surprise.

"Oh, my! How you startled me!" exclaimed the red squirrel. "But I'm glad it's you, Uncle Wiggily. I'm going to a surprise party soon, and I was just trying to make my tail as big as Johnnie or Billie Bushytail's, but I can't do it," she said sadly.

"No, and you never can," said the rabbit. "Their tails are a different kind than yours, for they are gray squirrels and you are a red one. But yours is very nice. Be content to have yours as it is."

"I guess I will," said the red squirrel. "But what are you doing out so late, Uncle Wiggily?"

"Looking for the end of the moon-beam to get my fortune."

"Ha! The moon-beam ends right here," said the red squirrel-girl, pointing to her looking-glass, and, surely enough, there the bright shaft of light ended. "But there is no fortune here, Uncle Wiggily, I am sorry to say," she added.

"I see there isn't," answered the rabbit. "Well, I must travel on again to-morrow, then. But now I will see that you get safely home, for it is getting late."

And, just as he said that, what should happen but that a black, savage, ugly bear stuck his nose out of the bushes and made a grab for the rabbit. But what do you think the red squirrel did?

She just took her hair brush and with the hard back of it she whacked the bear on the end of his tender-ender nose, and he howled, and turned around to run away, and the squirrel girl tickled him with the comb, and he ran faster than ever, and the bear didn't eat Uncle Wiggily that night.

Then the rabbit stayed at the red squirrel's mamma's house the rest of the evening, and the next day the squirrel went to the surprise party with her tail the regular size it ought to be, and not as big as the Bushytail brothers' tails, and everybody was happy.

Now in case the granddaddy longlegs doesn't tickle the baby with his long cow-pointing leg and make her laugh so she gets the hiccoughs, I'll tell you in the next story about Uncle Wiggily and the brown wren.

Howard R. Garis

STORY II

UNCLE WIGGILY AND THE BROWN WREN

Well, just as I expected, the granddaddy longlegs did tickle the baby, but she only smiled in her sleep, and didn't awaken, so, as it's nice and quiet I can tell you another story. And it's going to be about how Uncle Wiggily, in his travels about the country, in search of his fortune, helped a little brown wren.

"Well, where are you going this morning?" asked the red squirrel's mother as Uncle Wiggily finished his breakfast, and shook out from his long ears the oatmeal crumbs that had fallen in them.

"Oh, I suppose I will have to be traveling on," answered the rabbit. "That fortune of mine seems to be a long distance off. I've tried rainbows and moon-beams and I didn't find any money at their ends. I guess I'll have to look under the water next, but I'll wait until I get back home, and then I'll have Jimmie Wibblewobble the duck boy put his head at the bottom of the pond and see if there is any gold down there."

So off the old gentleman rabbit started, limping on his crutch, for his rheumatism was troubling him again, and at his side swung his valise, with some crackers and cheese and bread and butter and jam in it - plenty of jam, too, let me tell you, for the red squirrel's mamma could make lovely preserves, and this was carrot jam, with turnip frosting on it.

Well, Uncle Wiggily traveled on and on, over the hills and through the deep woods, and pretty soon he came to a place where he saw a lot of little black ants trying to carry to their nest a nice big piece of meat that some one had dropped.

"My, how hard those ants are working," thought the rabbit. "But that meat is too heavy for them. I'll have to help carry it."

Now the piece of meat was only as big as a quarter of a small cocoanut, but, of course, that's too big for an ant to carry; or even for forty-'leven ants, so Uncle Wiggily kindly lifted it for them, and put it in their nest.

"Thank you very much," said the biggest ant. "If ever we can do you a favor, or any of your friends, we will."

The old gentleman rabbit said he was glad to hear that, and then, taking up his crutch and valise again, on he went.

Pretty soon he came to a place in the woods where the sun was shining down through the trees, and a little brook was making pretty music over the stones. And then, all at once, the old gentleman rabbit heard a different kind of music, and it was that of a little bird singing. And this is the song.

Now I did not make up this song. It is much prettier than I could write, even if I had my Sunday-go-to-meeting clothes on, and I don't know who did write it. But it used to be in my school reader when I was a little boy, and I liked it very much. I hope whoever did write it won't mind if you sing it. This is it:

"There's a little brown bird sitting up in a tree,
He's singing to you - he's singing to me.
And what does he say, little girl - little boy?
Oh, the world's running over with joy!"

Then the bird sang about how there were five eggs laid away up in a nest, and how, pretty soon, little birds would come out from them, and then, all of a sudden, the bird sang like this:

"But don't meddle, - don't touch,
Little girl - little boy,
Or the world will lose some of its joy!"

"Ha! you seem quite happy this beautiful morning," said Uncle Wiggily, as he paused under the tree where the bird was singing. "Why, I do declare," he exclaimed. "If it isn't Mrs. Wren! Well, I never in all my born days! I didn't know you were back from the South yet."

"Yes, Uncle Wiggily," said the little brown wren, "I came up some time ago. But I'm real glad to see you. I'm going to take my little birdies out of the shell pretty soon. They are almost hatched."

"Glad to hear it," said the rabbit, politely, and then he told about seeking his fortune, and all of a sudden a great big ugly crow-bird flew down out of a tall tree and made a dash for Mrs. Wren to eat her up. But Mrs. Wren got out of the way just in time, and didn't get caught.

But alack, and alas-a-day! The crow knocked down the wren's nest, and all the sticks and feathers of which it was made were scattered all about, and the eggs, with the little birdies inside, would have been all broken ker-smash, only that they happened to fall down on some soft moss.

"Oh, dear!" cried Mrs. Wren, sorrowfully. "Now see what that crow has done! My home is broken up, and my birdies will be killed."

"Caw! Caw! Caw!" cried the crow as unkindly as he could, and it sounded just as if he laughed "Haw! Haw! Haw!"

"Oh, whatever shall I do?" asked Mrs. Wren. "My birdies will have no nest, and I haven't time to make another and break up the little fine sticks that I need and gather the feathers that are scattered all over. Oh, what shall I do? Soon my birdies will be out of the shells."

"Never fear!" said Uncle Wiggily, bravely. "I will help you. I'll gather the sticks for you."

"Oh, but you haven't time; you must be off seeking your fortune," answered the wren.

"Oh, I guess my fortune can wait. It has been waiting for me a long time, and it won't hurt to wait a bit longer. I'll get you the sticks," said the rabbit gentleman.

So while Mrs. Wren sat over the eggs to keep them warm with her fluffy feathers, Uncle Wiggily looked for sticks with which to make a new nest. He couldn't find any short and small enough, so what do you think he did?

Why, he took some big sticks and he jumped a jiggily dance up and down on them with his sharp paws, and broke them up as fine as toothpicks for the nest. Then he arranged them as well as he could in a sort of hollow, like a tea cup.

"Oh, if we only had some feathers now, we would be all right," said Mrs. Wren. "It's a very good nest for a rabbit to make."

"Don't say a word!" cried some small voices on the ground. "We will gather up the feathers for you." And there came marching up a lot of the little ants that Uncle Wiggily had been kind to, and soon they had gathered up all the scattered feathers. And the nest was made on a mossy stump, and lined with the feathers, and the warm eggs were put in it by Mrs. Wren, who then hovered over them to hatch out the birdies. And she was very thankful to Uncle Wiggily for what he had done.

Now, in case the water in the lake doesn't get inside the milk pail and make lemonade of it, I'll tell you in the next story how the birdies were hatched out, and also about Uncle Wiggily and the sunfish.

Howard R. Garis

STORY III

UNCLE WIGGILY AND THE SUNFISH

Uncle Wiggily slept that night - I mean the night after he had helped Mrs. Wren build her nest - he slept in an old underground house that another rabbit must have made some time before. It was nicely lined with leaves, and the fortune-hunting bunny slept very nice and warm there.

When the sun was up, shining very brightly, and most beautifully, Uncle Wiggily arose, shook his ears to get the dust out of them, and threw the dried-leaf blankets off him.

"Ah, ha! I must be up and doing," he cried. "Perhaps I shall find my fortune to-day."

Well, no sooner had he crawled out of the burrow than he heard a most beautiful song. It was one Mrs. Wren was singing, and it went "tra-la-la tra-la-la! tum-tee-tee-tum-tum-tee-tee!" too pretty for anything. And then, afterward, there was a sort of an echo like "cheep-cheep cheep-cheep!"

"Why, you must be very happy this morning, Mrs. Wren!" called Uncle Wiggily to her as she sat in her new nest which the rabbit had made for her on the mossy stump.

"I am," she answered, "very happy. What do you think happened in the night?"

"I can't guess," he answered. "A burglar crow didn't come and steal your eggs, I hope!"

"Oh, nothing sad or bad like that," she answered. "But something very nice. Just hop up here and look."

So Uncle Wiggily hopped up on the stump, and Mrs. Wren got off her nest, and there, on the bottom, in among some egg-shells, were a lot of tiny, weeny little birdies, about as big as a spool of silk thread or even smaller.

"Why, where in the world did they come from?" asked the old gentleman rabbit, rubbing his eyes.

"Out of the eggs to be sure," answered Mrs. Wren. "And I do declare, the last of my family is hatched now. There is little Wiggily out of the shell at last. I think I'll name him after you, as he never could keep still when he was being hatched. Now I must take out all the broken shells so the birdies won't cut themselves on them." And she began to throw them out with her bill, just as the mother hen does, and then one of the new little birdies called out:

"Cheep-cheep-chip-chip!"

"Yes, I know you're hungry," answered their mamma, who understood their bird talk. "Well, I'll fly away and get you something to eat just as soon as your papa comes home to stay in the house. You know Mr. Wren went away last night to see about getting a new position in a feather pillow factory," said Mrs. Wren to Uncle Wiggily, "and he doesn't yet know about the birdies. I hope he'll come back soon, as they are very hungry, and I don't like to leave them alone to go shopping."

"Oh, I'll stay and take care of them for you while you go to the store," said the old gentleman rabbit, kindly.

"That will do very well," said Mrs. Wren. So she put on her bonnet and shawl and took her market basket and off she flew to the store, while Uncle Wiggily stayed with the new birdies, and they snuggled down under his warm fur, and were as cozy as in their own mother's feathers.

Well, Mrs. Wren was gone some time, as the store was crowded and she couldn't get waited on right away, and Uncle Wiggily stayed with the birdies. And they got hungrier and hungrier, and they cried real hard. Yes, indeed, as hard as some babies.

"Hum! I don't know what to do," said the old gentleman rabbit. "I can't feed them. I guess I'll sing to them." So he sang this song:

"Hush, birdies, hush,
Please don't cry;
Mamma'll be back
By and by.

"Nestle down close
Under my fur,
I'm not your mother, but
I'm helping her."

But this didn't seem to satisfy the birdies and they cried "cheep-cheep" harder than ever.

"Oh, dear! I believe I must get them something to eat," said Uncle Wiggily. So he covered them all up warmly with the feathers that lined the nest, and then he hopped down and went limping around on his crutch to find them something to eat.

Pretty soon he came to a little brook, and as he looked down into it he saw something shining, all gold and red and green and blue and yellow.

"Why, I do declare, if here isn't the end of the rainbow!" exclaimed the old gentleman rabbit, as he saw all the pretty colors.

He rubbed his eyes with his paw, to make sure he wasn't dreaming, but the colors were surely enough there, down under water.

"No wonder the giant couldn't find the pot of gold, it was down in the water," spoke the rabbit. "But I'll get it, and then my fortune will be made. Oh, how glad I am!"

Well, Uncle Wiggily reached his paw down and made a grab for the red and green and gold and yellow thing, but to his surprise, instead of lifting up a pot of gold, he lifted up a squirming, wiggling sunfish.

"Oh, my!" exclaimed the rabbit in surprise.

"I should say yes! Two Oh mys and another one!" gasped the fish. "Oh, please put me back in the water again. The air out on land is too strong for me. I can't breathe. Please, Uncle Wiggily, put me back."

"I thought you were a pot of gold," said the rabbit, sadly. "I'm always getting fooled. But never mind. I'll put you in the water."

"What are you doing here?" asked the fish, as he slid into the water again and sneezed three times.

"Just at present I am taking care of Mrs. Wren's new little birdies," said the rabbit. "She has gone to the store for something for them to eat, but they are so hungry they can't wait."

"Oh, that is easily fixed," said the sunfish. "Since you were so kind to me I'll tell you what to do. Get them a few little worms, and some small flower seeds, and feed them. Then the birdies will go to sleep."

So Uncle Wiggily did this, and as soon as the birds had their hungry little mouths filled, sound to sleep they went. And in a

Howard R. Garis

little while Mrs. Wren came back from the store with her basket filled, and Mr. Wren flew home to say that he had a nice position in a feather factory, and how he did admire his birdies! He hugged and kissed them like anything.

Then the two wrens both thanked Uncle Wiggily for taking care of their children, and the rabbit said good-by and hopped on again to seek his fortune. And if the trolley car conductor gives me a red, white and blue transfer, for the pin cushion to go to sleep on, I'll tell you in the following story about Uncle Wiggily and the yellow bird.

STORY IV

UNCLE WIGGILY AND THE YELLOW BIRD

Once upon a time, when Johnnie Bushytail was going along the road to school, he met a fox - oh, just listen to me, would you! This story isn't about the squirrel boy at all. It's about Uncle Wiggily Longears to be sure, and the yellow bird, so I must begin all over again.

The day after the old gentleman rabbit had helped Mrs. Wren feed her little birdies he found himself traveling along a lonely road through a big forest of tall trees. Oh, it was a very lonesome place, and not even an automobile was to be seen, and there wasn't the smell of gasoline, and no "honk-honks" to waken the baby from her sleep.

"Hum, I don't believe I'll find any fortune along here," thought Uncle Wiggily as he tramped on. "I haven't met even so much as a red ant, or even a black one, or a grasshopper. I wonder if I can be lost?"

So he looked all around to see if he might be lost in the woods. But you know how it is, sometimes you're lost when you least expect it, and again you think you are lost, but you're right near home all the while.

That's the way it was with Uncle Wiggily, he didn't know whether or not he was lost, so he thought he'd sit down on a flat stone and eat his lunch. The reason he sat on a flat stone

Howard R. Garis

instead of a round one was because he had some hard boiled eggs for his lunch, and you know if you put an egg on a round stone it's bound to roll off and crack right in the middle.

"And I don't like cracked eggs," said the rabbit. So he laid the eggs he had on the flat stone, and put little sticks in front of them and behind them, so they couldn't even roll off the flat stone if they wanted to. Then he ate his lunch.

"I guess it doesn't much matter if I am lost," said the traveling fortune-hunting rabbit a little later. "I'll go on and perhaps I may meet with an adventure." So on he hopped, and pretty soon he came to a place where the leaves and the dirt were all torn up, just as if some boys had been playing a baseball game, or leap-frog, or something like that.

"My, I must look out that I don't tumble down any holes here," thought Uncle Wiggily, "for maybe some bad men have been setting traps to catch us rabbits."

Well, he turned to one side, to get out of the way of some sharp thorns, and, my goodness! if there weren't more sharp thorns on the ground on the other side of the path. "I guess I'll have to keep straight ahead!" thought our Uncle Wiggily. "I never saw so many thorns before in all my life. I'll have to look out or I'll be stuck."

So he kept straight on, and all of a sudden he felt himself going down into a big hole.

"Oh! Oh dear! Oh me! Oh my!" cried Uncle Wiggily. "I've fallen into a trap! That's what those thorns were for - so I would have to walk toward the trap instead of going to one side."

But, very luckily for Uncle Wiggily, his crutch happened to catch across the hole, and so he didn't go all the way down, but hung on. But his valise fell to the bottom. However, he managed to pull himself up on the ground, though his rheumatism hurt him, and soon he was safe once more.

"Oh, my valise, with all my clothes in it!" he cried, as he looked down into the hole, which had been covered over with loose leaves and dirt so he couldn't see it before falling in. "I wonder how I can get my things back again?" he went on.

Then he looked up, and in a tree, not far from him, he saw something bright and yellow, shining like gold.

"Ah, ha!" cried Uncle Wiggily. "At last I have found the pot of gold, even if the rainbow isn't here. That is yellow, and yellow is the color of gold. Now my fortune is made. I will get that gold and go back home."

So, not worrying any more about his valise down the trap-hole, Uncle Wiggily hopped over to the tree to get what he thought was a big bunch of yellow gold. But as he came closer, he saw that the gold was moving about and fluttering, though not going very far away.

"That is queer gold," thought the old gentleman rabbit. "I never saw moving gold before. I wonder if it is a good kind."

Then he went a little closer and he heard a voice crying.

"Why, that is crying gold, too," he said. "This is very strange."

Then he heard some one calling:

"Oh, help! Will some one please help me?"

"Why, this is most strange of all!" the rabbit cried. "It is talking gold. Perhaps there is a fairy about."

"Oh, I only wish there was one!" cried the yellow object in the tree. "If I saw a fairy I'd ask her to set me free."

"What's that? Who are you?" asked the rabbit.

Howard R. Garis

"Oh, I'm a poor little yellow bird," was the answer, "and I'm caught in a string-trap that some boys set in this tree. There is a string around my legs and I can't fly home to see my little ones. I got into the trap by mistake. Oh! can't you help me? Climb up into the tree, Uncle Wiggily, and help me!"

"How did you know my name was Uncle Wiggily?" asked the rabbit.

"I could tell it by your ears - your wiggling ears," was the answer. "But please climb up and help me."

"Rabbits can't climb trees," said Uncle Wiggily. "But I will tell you what I'll do. I'll gnaw the tree down with my sharp teeth, for they are sharp, even if I am a little old. Then, when it falls, I can reach the string, untie it, and you will be free."

So Uncle Wiggily did this, and soon the tree fell down, but the golden yellow bird was on a top branch and didn't get hurt. Then the old gentleman rabbit quickly untied the string and the bird was out of the trap.

"I cannot thank you enough!" she said to the rabbit. "Is there anything I can do for you to pay you?"

"Well, my valise is down a hole," said Uncle Wiggily, "but I don't see how you can get it up. I need it, though."

"I can fly down, tie the string to the satchel and you can pull it up," said the birdie. And she did so, and the rabbit pulled up his valise as nicely as a bucket of water is hoisted up from the well. Then some bad boys and a man came along to see if there was anything in the hole-trap, or the string-trap they had made; but when they saw the bird flying away and the rabbit hopping away through the woods they were very angry. But Uncle Wiggily and the yellow bird were safe from harm, I'm glad to say.

And the rabbit had another adventure soon after that, and

what it was I'll tell you soon, when the story will be about
Uncle Wiggily and the skyrockets. It will be a Fourth of July
story, if you please; that is if the bean bag doesn't fall down the
coal hole and catch a mosquito.

Howard R. Garis

STORY V

UNCLE WIGGILY AND THE SKY-CRACKER

Let me see, I think I promised to tell you a story about Uncle Wiggily and the skyrocket, didn't I? Or was it to be about a firecracker, seeing that it soon may be the Fourth of July? What's that - a firecracker - no? A skyrocket? Oh, I'm all puzzled up about it, so I guess I'll make it a sky-cracker, a sort of half-firecracker and half-skyrocket, and that will do.

Well, after Uncle Wiggily had gotten the little yellow bird, that looked like gold, out from the string-trap in the tree, the old gentleman rabbit spent two nights visiting a second cousin of Grandfather Prickly Porcupine, who lived in the woods. Then Uncle Wiggily got up one morning, dressed himself very carefully, combed out his whiskers, and said:

"Well, I'm off again to seek my fortune."

"It's too bad you can't seem able to find it," said the second cousin to Grandfather Prickly Porcupine, "but perhaps you will have good luck to-day. Only you want to be very careful."

"Why?" asked the old gentleman rabbit.

"Well, because you know it will soon be the Fourth of July, and some boys may tie a firecracker or a skyrocket to your tail," said the porcupine.

"Ha! Ha!" laughed Uncle Wiggily. "They will have a hard time doing that, for my tail is so short that the boys would burn their fingers if they tried to tie a firecracker to it."

"Then look out that they don't fasten a skyrocket to your long ears," said the second cousin to Grandfather Prickly Porcupine, as he wrapped up some lettuce and carrot sandwiches for Uncle Wiggily to take with him.

The old gentleman rabbit said he would watch out, and away he started, going up hill and down hill with his barber-pole crutch as easily as if he was being wheeled in a baby carriage.

"Well, I don't seem to find any fortune," he said to himself as he walked along, and, just as he said that he saw something sparkling in the grass beside the path in the woods. "What's that?" he cried. "Perhaps it is a diamond. If it is I can sell it and get rich." Then he happened to think what the second cousin of Grandfather Prickly Porcupine had told him about Fourth of July coming, and Uncle Wiggily said:

"Ha! I had better be careful. Perhaps that sparkling thing is a spark on a firecracker. Ah, ha!"

So he looked more carefully, and the bright object sparkled more and more, and it didn't seem to be fire, so the old gentleman rabbit went up close, and what do you suppose it was?

Why, it was a great big dewdrop, right in the middle of a purple violet, that was growing underneath a shady fern. Oh, how beautiful it was in the sunlight, and Uncle Wiggily was glad he had looked at it. And pretty soon, as he was still looking, a big, buzzing bumble bee buzzed along and stopped to take a sip of the dewdrop.

"Ha! That is a regular violet ice cream soda for me!" said the bee to Uncle Wiggily. And just as he was taking another drink a big, ugly snake made a spring and tried to eat the bee, but Uncle Wiggily hit the snake with his crutch and the snake

Howard R. Garis

crawled away very much surprised.

"Thank you very much," said the bee to the rabbit. "You saved my life, and if ever I can do you a favor I will," and with that he buzzed away.

Well, pretty soon, not so very long, in a little while, Uncle Wiggily came to a place in the woods where there were a whole lot of packages done up in paper lying on the ground. And there was a tent near them, and it looked as if people lived in the white tent, only no one was there just then.

"I guess I'd better keep away," thought the old gentleman rabbit, "or they may catch me." And just then he saw something like a long, straight stick, standing up against a tree. "Ha, that will be a good stick to take along to chase the bears away with," he thought. "I think no one wants it, so I'll take it."

Well, he walked up and took hold of it in his paws, but, mind you, he didn't notice that on one end of the stick was a piece of powder string, like the string of a firecracker, sticking down, and this string was burning. No, the poor old gentleman, rabbit never noticed that at all. He started to take the stick away with him when, all of a sudden, something dreadful happened.

With a whizz and a rush and a roar that stick shot into the air, carrying Uncle Wiggily with it, just like a balloon, for he hadn't time to let go of it.

Up and up he went, with a roar and a swoop, and just then he saw a whole lot of boys rushing out of the woods toward the white tent. And one boy cried:

"Oh, fellows, look! A rabbit has hold of our sky-cracker and it's on fire and has gone off and taken him with it! Oh the poor rabbit! Because when the sky-cracker gets high enough in the air the firecracker part of it will go off with a bang, and he'll be killed. Oh, how sorry I am. The hot sun must have set fire to the powder string."

You see those boys had come out in the woods to have their Fourth of July, where the noise wouldn't make any one's head ache.

Well, Uncle Wiggily went on, up and up, with the sky-cracker, and he felt very much afraid for he had heard what the boys said.

"Oh, this is the end of me!" he cried, as he held fast to the sky-cracker. "I'll never live to find my fortune now. When this thing explodes, I'll be dashed to the ground and killed."

The sky-cracker was whizzing and roaring, and black smoke was pouring out of one end, and Uncle Wiggily thought of all his friends whom he feared he would never see again, when all of a sudden along came flying the buzzing bumble bee, high in the air. He was much surprised to see Uncle Wiggily skimming along on the tail of a sky-cracker.

"Oh, can't you save me?" cried the rabbit.

"Indeed I will, if I can," said the bee, "because you were so kind to me. You are too heavy, or I would fly down to earth with you myself, but I'll do the next best thing. I'll fly off and get Dickie and Nellie Chip-Chip, the sparrow children, and they'll come with a big basket and catch you so you won't fall."

No sooner said than done. Off flew the bee. Quickly he found Dickie and Nellie and told them the danger Uncle Wiggily was in.

"Quick," called Dickie to Nellie. "We must save him."

Off they flew like the wind, carrying a grocery basket between them. Right under Uncle Wiggily they flew, and just as the sky-cracker was going to burst with a "slam-bang!" the old gentleman rabbit let go, and into the basket he safely fell and the sparrow children flew to earth with him. Then the sky-cracker burst all to pieces for Fourth of July, but Uncle Wiggily wasn't on it to be hurt, I'm glad to say.

He spent the Fourth visiting the Bumble bee's family, and had ice cream and cake and lemonade for supper, and at night he heard the band play, and he gave Nellie and Dickie ten cents for ice cream sodas, and that's all to this story.

But on the next page, if the baker man brings me a pound of soap bubbles with candy in the middle for Cora Janet's doll, I'll tell you about Uncle Wiggily and the buttercup.

STORY VI

UNCLE WIGGILY AND THE BUTTERCUP

I hope none of you were burned by a sky-cracker or a Roman candle stick when you had your Fourth of July celebration, but if you were I hope you will soon be better, and perhaps if I tell you a story it will make you forget the pain. So here we go, all about Uncle Wiggily and the buttercup.

The old gentleman rabbit spent a few days in an old burrow next to the bumble bee's house, and then one morning, when the sun was shining brightly, he started off again to seek his fortune.

"I never can thank you enough," he said to the bee, "for going after the sparrow children and saving me from the exploding sky-cracker. If ever I find my fortune I will give you some of it."

"Thank you very kindly," said the bee, as she looked in the pantry, "and here are some sweet honey sandwiches for you to eat on your travels. This is some honey that I made myself."

"Then it must be very good," said the old gentleman rabbit politely, as he put the sandwiches in his valise and started off down the dusty road.

Well, he hopped on and on, sometimes in the woods where it was cool and green and shady, and sometimes out in the hot

Howard R. Garis

sun, and every minute or so he would stop and look around to see if he could find his fortune.

"For, who knows?" he said, "perhaps I may pick up a bag of gold, or some diamonds at almost any minute. Then I could go back home and buy an automobile for myself to ride around in, and my travels would be over. I have certainly been on the go a long time, but my health is much better than it was."

So he kept on, looking under all the big leaves and clumps of ferns for his fortune. But he didn't find it, and pretty soon he came to a hole in the ground. And in front of this hole was a little sign, printed on a piece of paper, and it read:

"COME IN! EVERYBODY WELCOME."

"Humph! I wonder if that means me?" thought the old gentleman rabbit. "Let's see, gold grows under ground, in mines, and perhaps this is a gold mine. I'm going down. I'm sure there is a fortune waiting for me. Yes, I'll go down."

So he laid aside his valise and barber-pole crutch and got ready to go down in the hole, which wasn't very big.

"But I can scratch it bigger if I need to," said Uncle Wiggily.

Well, he had no sooner gotten his front feet and part of his nose down the hole, but his ears were still sticking out, when he heard a voice calling:

"Here! Where are you going?"

"Down this hole after gold," replied Uncle Wiggily.

"You mustn't go down there," went on the voice, and pulling out his nose and looking about him, the old gentleman rabbit saw a white pussy cat sitting on a stump. And the pussy cat was washing his face with his paws, taking care not to let the claws stick out for fear of scratching his eyes.

"Why can't I go down this hole, Pussy?" asked the rabbit. "Do you have charge of it?"

"No, indeed," was the answer, "but there is a bad snake who lives down there, and he puts up that sign so the animals will come down, and then he eats them. That's the reason he says they are welcome. No, indeed, I wouldn't want to see you go down there!"

"Ha! Hum! I wouldn't like to see myself!" spoke Uncle Wiggily, and he crawled away from the hole just in time, for the snake stuck out his ugly head and was about to bite the rabbit. It was the same snake that had nearly caught the bumble bee.

"Say!" cried the snake, quite angry like, to the pussy cat, "I wish you would get away from here! You are always spoiling my plans. I thought I was going to have a nice rabbit dinner, and now look at what you have done," and that snake was so angry that he hissed like a boiling teakettle.

"I will never let you eat up Uncle Wiggily!" cried the pussy. "Now look out for yourself, Mr. Snake!" and with that the pussy made his back round like a hoop, and he swelled up his tail like a bologna sausage, and he showed his teeth and claws to the snake, and that snake popped down the hole again very quickly, I can tell you, taking his tail with him. Oh, my, yes, and a bucket of sawdust soup besides.

"I thank you very much for telling me about that snake, little pussy cat," said Uncle Wiggily. "Well, I am disappointed about my fortune again. I shall never be rich I fear. But I almost forgot that I have some fine honey sandwiches and I will give you some, for you must be hungry. I know I am."

"I am, too," said the pussy. So Uncle Wiggily opened his valise and took out the honey sandwiches which the bee had given

Howard R. Garis

him, but when he went to eat them he found that the bee had forgotten to butter the bread.

"Oh, that is too bad!" cried the pussy, when Uncle Wiggily spoke of it. "Still they will do very well without butter."

"No, we must have some," said the rabbit. "I wonder how I can get butter in the woods?" So he looked all around and the first thing he saw was a yellow buttercup flower. You know the kind I mean. You hold them under your chin to see if you like butter, and the shine of the flower makes your chin yellow.

"Ha!" exclaimed Uncle Wiggily. "Now we will have butter."

"But you are not going to eat the flower, are you?" asked the pussy.

"No, indeed!" cried the rabbit, "I'll show you."

Now there was a cow in the field a short distance away, and Uncle Wiggily went over and got some milk from the cow in a little tin cup. "Butter is made from milk," said the rabbit to the pussy. "So I will just pour some milk in the buttercup flower, and shake it just as if it was a churn, and then we'll have butter for our honey sandwiches."

So he did this. Into the buttercup he poured the milk, and it became yellow like butter at once. But Uncle Wiggily did not have to shake the flower, for a little wind came along just then and shook it for him.

And pretty soon, in a little while, the milk in the buttercup was churned into lovely sweet butter, and the rabbit and pussy spread it on their honey sandwiches, and what a fine feast they had. Just as they were eating it the bad alligator came along, and wanted to take the honey away from them, but the pussy scratched the end of the savage beast's tail with his claws, and the bad alligator ran away as fast as he could.

Then Uncle Wiggily and the pussy traveled on together and the next day they had quite an adventure. What it was I'll tell you in the next story when, in case the steamboat stops at our house for a little girl wearing a green sunbonnet, with horse chestnuts on it, I'll tell you about Uncle Wiggily and the July bug.

Howard R. Garis

STORY VII

UNCLE WIGGILY AND THE JULY BUG

"Well, what shall we do to-day?" asked the white pussy of Uncle Wiggily, as they traveled on together, the next day after the adventure at the snake hole. They had slept that night in a nice hollow stump.

"Hum! I hardly know what to do," replied the old gentleman rabbit. "Of course I must be on the watch for my fortune, but, as I don't seem to be finding it very fast, what do you say to having a picnic to-day?"

"The very thing!" cried pussy. "We will get some lunch, and go off in the woods and eat it. Only we ought to have a lot more people. Two are hardly enough for a picnic."

"I would like some of my friends to come to it," spoke Uncle Wiggily, "but I am afraid they are too far off."

"Couldn't you send them word by telephone?" inquired the pussy. "I'm sure I would like to meet them, for I have heard so much about Sammie and Susie Littletail, and Johnnie and Billie Bushytail."

"There is no telephone in these woods," replied Uncle Wiggily, "and we haven't time to send them postcards. I wish I could get word to them, however, but I don't s'pose I can."

"Yes, you can!" suddenly cried a voice down in the grass. "I'll tell all your friends to come to the picnic if you like."

"Indeed, I would like it," said the rabbit, "but who are you, if I may be so bold as to ask? I can't see you."

"There he is - it's a big June bug!" exclaimed the pussy.

"I beg your pardon," spoke the bug quickly, as he crawled out from under a leaf and sat on a toadstool. "But I am not a June bug, if you please."

"You look like one," said Uncle Wiggily politely.

"I am a July bug," went on the funny little creature. "I was intended for a June bug, but there was some mistake made, and I didn't come out of my shell until July. So you see I'm a July bug, and at first I thought it would be jolly fun, to hear all the firecrackers and skyrockets go off."

"It isn't so much fun as you imagine," said Uncle Wiggily, as he thought of the time he went sailing into the air on the sky-cracker. "But don't you like being a July bug?"

"Not very much. You see I'm the only one there is, and all the others are June bugs. The June bugs won't speak to me, nor let me play with them, so I'm very lonesome. I heard you talking about a picnic you were going to have, and so I offered to call all your friends to it. I thought perhaps if I did that you would let me come to it also."

"To be sure!" exclaimed Uncle Wiggily. "You may gladly come, but how are you going to send word to all of my friends?"

"I will fly through the air and tell them to come," was the answer. "I am a very swift flyer. Watch me," and then and there the July bug buzzed around so fast that Uncle Wiggily and the pussy couldn't see his wings go flip-flop-flap.

Howard R. Garis

Well, they decided it would be a good plan to have the July bug act as a postman, so Uncle Wiggily wrote out the invitations on little pieces of white birch bark, and gave them to the bug. Off he flew into the air waving one leg at Uncle Wiggily and the pussy.

"Well, now we must get ready for the picnic - get the things to eat - for that bug flies so fast that soon all my friends will be here," said the rabbit, so he and the pussy began to get the lunch ready.

Uncle Wiggily had some food in his valise, but they got more good things from a kind old monkey who lived in the woods. He used to work on a hand organ, but when he got old he bought him a nest in the woods with the pennies he had saved up, and he lived in peace and quietness, and played a mouth organ on Sundays.

Well, you will hardly believe me, but it's true, no sooner had Uncle Wiggily and the pussy put up the lunch, wrapping some for each visitor in nice, green grape leaves, than the first ones of the picnic party began to arrive. They were Dickie and Nellie Chip-Chip, the sparrows, for they could fly through the air very quickly, and so they came on ahead.

"We got your invitation that the July bug left us, Uncle Wiggily, and we came at once," said Dickie.

"Where are the others?" asked the old gentleman rabbit.

"They are coming," answered Nellie, as she tied her tail ribbon over again, for the bow knot had become undone as she was flying through the air.

Well, in a little while along came hopping, Sammie and Susie Littletail, the rabbit children, and Billie and Johnnie Bushytail, the squirrel brothers, and Bully and Bawly the frogs, and Dottie and Munchie Trot, the ponies, and Lulu and Alice and Jimmie Wibblewobble, the duck twins, and Buddy and

Brighteyes Pigg, and oh, all the boy and girl animals I have ever told you about.

And oh! how glad they were to see Uncle Wiggily. He had to tell them all about his travels after his fortune before they would go off in the woods to the picnic. But at last they went, each one with a little leaf-package of lunch. The July bug came along, too, and he had a very little package of good things, because he was so small, you see, but it was enough.

They all sat down on the ground with flat stones for plates, and sticks for knives and forks, and they ate their picnic lunch there. Oh, they had the finest time, and it didn't matter if some ants did get in the sugar. Uncle Wiggily said they could have all they wanted of the sweet stuff.

And, when the picnic was almost over, there was a sudden noise in the bushes, and two bad foxes sprang out. One tried to grab Uncle Wiggily, and another made a dash for Lulu Wibblewobble.

"Oh dear!" cried Dottie Trot, without looking to see if her hair ribbon was on straight. "We shall all be eaten up!"

"No, you won't!" cried the brave July bug. "I'll fix those foxes!"

So that brave July bug just buzzed his wings as hard as he could, and straight at those foxes he flew, bumping and banging them on their noses and in the eyes, so that they gave two separate and distinct howls, and ran away, taking their big tails with them.

So that is how the July bug saved everybody from being eaten up, and then the picnic was over and every one said it was lovely.

"Well, I'll start on my travels again to-morrow," said Uncle Wiggily, as his friends told him good-by.

Howard R. Garis

Now what happened to him the next day I'll tell you very soon, for, in case I see a chipmunk with a blue tail and a red nose climbing up the clothes pole, the story will be about Uncle Wiggily and Jack-in-the-pulpit.

STORY VIII

UNCLE WIGGILY AND JACK-IN-THE-PULPIT

Uncle Wiggily was slowly hopping along through the woods, sometimes leaning on his crutch, when his rheumatism pained him, and again skipping along when he got out into the warm sunshine. It was the day after the picnic, and the old gentleman rabbit felt a bit lonesome as all his friends had gone back to their homes.

"I do declare!" exclaimed Uncle Wiggily, as he walked slowly along by a little lake, where an August rabbit was running his motor boat, "if I don't find my fortune pretty soon I won't have any vacation this year. I must look carefully to-day, and see if I can't find a pot full of gold."

Well, he looked as carefully as he could, but my land sakes and a pair of white gloves! he couldn't seem to find a smitch of gold and not so much as a crumb of diamonds.

"Hum!" exclaimed Uncle Wiggily, "at this rate I guess I'll have to keep on traveling for several years before I find my fortune. But never mind, I'm having a good time, anyhow. I'll keep on searching."

So he kept on, and all of a sudden when he was walking past a prickly briar bush, he heard a voice calling:

"Hey, Uncle Wiggily, come on in here."

"Ha! Who are you, and why do you want me to come in there?" asked the old gentleman rabbit.

"Oh, I am a friend of yours," was the answer, "and I will give you a lot of money if you come in here."

"Let me see your face," asked the rabbit, "I want to know who you are."

"Oh! I have a dreadful toothache," said the creature hiding in the bushes. "I don't want to stick my face out in the cold. But if you will take my word for it I am a good friend of yours. I would like very much for you to come in here."

"Well, perhaps I had better," said the old gentleman rabbit, "for I certainly need money."

And he was just going to crawl in under the prickly briar bush when all of a sudden he happened to look, and he saw the skillery-scallery tail of the alligator accidentally sticking out. Yes, it was the alligator trying to fool dear old Uncle Wiggily.

"Oh, ho!" cried the wise old rabbit. "I guess I won't go in there after all," so he hopped to one side and the alligator kept waiting for him to come in so he could eat him, but when the rabbit didn't come in the savage creature with the skillery-scallery tail cried:

"Well, aren't you coming in?"

"No, thank you," said the rabbit. "I have to go on to seek my fortune," and away he hopped. Well, that alligator was so angry that he gnashed his teeth and nearly broke them, and he crawled after Uncle Wiggily, but of course, he couldn't catch him.

Uncle Wiggily was pretty careful after that, and whenever he came near a prickly briar bush he listened with both his long ears stuck up straight to see if he could hear any sounds like an alligator. But he didn't, and so he kept on.

Well, it was coming on toward evening, one afternoon, and the old gentleman rabbit was tramping along the road, wondering where he would sleep, when all of a sudden something came bursting out of the bushes toward the rabbit, and a voice cried out:

"Hide! Hide! Uncle Wiggily. Hide as quickly as you can!"

"Why should I hide?" asked the old gentleman rabbit. "Is there a giant coming after me?"

"Worse than a giant," said the voice. "It is a bad wolf that jumped out of his cage from the circus, and he is just ready to eat up anything he sees," and the July bug, for it was he who had fluttered out of the bushes, to tell Uncle Wiggily, made his wings go slowly to and fro like an electric palm-leaf fan.

"A wolf, eh?" cried the old gentleman rabbit. "And do you think he will eat me?"

"He surely will," said the July bug. "I happened to fly past his house, and I heard him say to his wife that he was going out to see if he could find a rabbit supper. So I know he's coming for you. You'd better hide."

"Oh! where can I hide?" asked the rabbit, as he looked around for a hollow stump. But there wasn't any, and there were no holes in the ground, and he didn't know what to do.

Then, all at once there was a crashing in the bushes and it sounded like an elephant coming through, breaking all the sticks in his path.

"There's the wolf! There's the wolf!" cried the July bug. "Hide, Uncle Wiggily," and then the bug perched on the high limb of a tree where the wolf couldn't catch him.

Howard R. Garis

Well, the poor old gentleman rabbit looked for a place to hide himself away from the wolf but he couldn't seem to find any, and he was just going to crawl under a stone and maybe hurt himself, when all at once he heard a voice say:

"Jump up here, Uncle Wiggily. I'll hide you from the wolf."

So the rabbit traveler looked up, and there he saw a flower called Jack-in-the-pulpit looking down on him. I've told you about them before, how the frog once took his bath in one, and how, when you pick a wood-bouquet you put them in with some ferns to make the bouquet look pretty. They are a flower like a vase, with a top curling over, and a thing standing up in the centre whose name is "Jack."

"Jump in here," said the Jack. "I'll fold my top down over you like an umbrella, and the wolf can't find you."

"But you are so small that I can't get inside," said the rabbit.

"Oh, I'll make myself bigger," cried the Jack, I and he took a long breath, and puffed himself up and swelled himself up, until he was large enough for Uncle Wiggily to jump down inside. Then the Jack-in-the-pulpit closed down the umbrella top over the rabbit, and he was hidden away as nice and snug as could be wished.

Pretty soon that bad savage wolf came prancing along, and he looked all over for the rabbit. Then he sniffed and cried:

"Ha! I smell him somewhere around here! I'll find him!" But he couldn't see Uncle Wiggily because he was safely hidden in the Jack-in-the-pulpit. So the wolf raged around some more and chased after his tail, and just as he smelled the rabbit hidden in the flower, the July bug flew down out of the tree, bang! right into the eyes of the wolf, and then the savage creature felt so badly that he ran home and ate cold bread and water for supper, and he didn't bother Uncle Wiggily any more that day.

So that's how the Jack-in-the-pulpit saved the rabbit and very thankful Uncle Wiggily was. And he stayed that night in a hollow stump, and the next day he went on to seek his fortune.

And quite a curious thing happened to him, as I shall have the pleasure of telling you about soon, when in case our canoe boat doesn't turn upside down and spill out the breakfast oatmeal, the next bedtime story will be about Uncle Wiggily and the lost chipmunk.

Howard R. Garis

STORY IX

UNCLE WIGGILY AND THE LOST CHIPMUNK

Uncle Wiggily was walking along the road one morning, after he had slept all night in the hollow stump. He didn't have any breakfast either, for there was nothing left in his valise, and of course he couldn't eat his barber-pole crutch. If the crutch had had a hole in it, like in the elephant's trunk, then the old gentleman rabbit could have carried along some sandwiches. But, as it was, he had nothing for breakfast, and he hadn't had much supper either, the night before.

"Oh, how hungry I am!" exclaimed Uncle Wiggily. "If only I had a piece of cherry pie now, or an ice cream cone, or a bit of bread and butter and jam I would be all right."

Well, he just happened to open his valise, and there on the very bottom, among some papers he found a few crumbs of the honey sandwiches the bumble bee had given him. Well, you never can imagine how good those few crumbs tasted to the old gentleman rabbit, which shows you that it is a good thing to be hungry once in a while, because even common things taste good.

But the crumbs weren't enough for Uncle Wiggily. As he walked along he kept getting hungrier and hungrier and he didn't know how he was going to stand it.

Then, all of a sudden, as he was passing by a hollow stump, he saw a whole lot of little black creatures crawling around it. They were going up and down, and they were very busy.

"Why, these are ants," said the rabbit. "Well, I s'pose they have plenty to eat. I almost wish I was an ant."

"Well! Well!" exclaimed a voice all at once. "If here isn't Uncle Wiggily. Where did you come from?" and there stood a second cousin to the ant for whom Uncle Wiggily had once carried home a pound of beefsteak with mushrooms on it.

"Oh, I am traveling about seeking my fortune," said the rabbit. "But I haven't been very successful. I couldn't even find my breakfast this morning."

"That's too bad!" exclaimed the ant who wore glasses. "We can give you something, however. Come on! everybody, help get breakfast for Uncle Wiggily."

So all the ants came running up, and some of them brought pieces of boiled eggs, and others brought oatmeal and others parts of oranges and still others parts of cups of coffee. So take it altogether, with seventeen million, four hundred and seventeen thousand, one hundred and eighty-five ants and a baby ant to wait on him, Uncle Wiggily managed to make out a pretty fair sort of a breakfast.

Well, after the old gentleman rabbit had eaten all the breakfast he could, he thanked the kind ants and said good-by to them. Then he started off again. He hadn't gone on very far through the woods, before, all of a sudden he saw something bright and shining under a blackberry bush.

"Well, I do declare!" cried the old gentleman rabbit. "I think that looks like gold. I hope I'm not fooled this time. I will go up very slowly and carefully. Perhaps I shall find my fortune now."

So up he walked very softly, and he stooped down and picked

Howard R. Garis

up the shining thing. And what do you think it was? Why a bright new penny - as shiny as gold.

"Good luck!" cried Uncle Wiggily, "I am beginning to find money. Soon I will be rich, and then I can stop traveling," and he put the penny in his pocket.

Well, no sooner had he done so than he heard some one crying over behind a raspberry bush. Oh, such a sad cry as it was, and the old gentleman rabbit knew right away that some one was in trouble.

"Who is there?" he asked, as he felt in his pocket to see if his penny was safe, for he thought that was the beginning of his fortune.

"Oh, I'm lost!" cried the voice. "I came to the store to buy a chocolate lollypop, and I can't find my way back," and then out from behind the raspberry bush came a tiny, little striped chipmunk with the tears falling down on her little paws.

"Oh, you poor little dear!" cried Uncle Wiggily. "And so you are lost? Well, don't you know what to do? As soon as you are lost you must go to a policeman and ask him to take you home. Policemen always know where everybody lives."

"But there are no policemen here," said the chipmunk, who was something like a squirrel, only smaller.

"That's so," agreed Uncle Wiggily. "Well, pretend that I am a policeman, and I'll take you home. Where do you live?"

"If I knew," said the chipmunk, "I would go home myself. All that I know is that I live in a hollow stump."

"Hum!" exclaimed Uncle Wiggily. "There are so many hollow stumps here, that I can't tell which one it is. We will go to each one, and when you find the one that is your home, just tell me."

"But that is not the worst," said the chipmunk. "I have lost my bright, new penny that my mamma gave me for a chocolate lollypop. Oh dear. Isn't it terrible."

"Perhaps this is your penny," said the old gentleman rabbit a bit sadly, taking from his pocket the one he had found.

"It is the very one!" cried the lost chipmunk, joyfully. "Oh, how good of you to find it for me."

"Well," thought Uncle Wiggily with a sorrowful sigh as he handed over the penny, "I thought I had found the beginning of my fortune, but I've lost it again. Never mind. I'll try to-morrow."

So he gave the penny to the chipmunk, and she stopped crying right away, and took hold of Uncle Wiggily's paw, and he led her around to all the hollow stumps until she found the right one where she lived.

And he bought her an ice cream cone because he felt sorry for her. And, just as she was eating it, along came a big, black bear and he wanted half of it, but very luckily the July bug flew past just then, and he bit the bear in the eyes, so that the bad bear was glad enough to run home, taking his little stumpy tail with him. Then the chipmunk took Uncle Wiggily back to her home, and he stayed with her papa and mamma all night.

Now, in case the rocking chair on our porch doesn't tip over in the middle of the night, and scare the pussy cat off the railing, I'll tell you next about Uncle Wiggily and the black cricket.

Howard R. Garis

STORY X

UNCLE WIGGILY AND THE BLACK CRICKET

Uncle Wiggily, the nice old gentleman rabbit, was feeling quite sad one morning as he hopped along the dusty road. It was a few days after he had helped the lost chipmunk find her way back home, and he had given her the lost penny which he had also picked up.

"Oh, dear me!" exclaimed Uncle Wiggily, as he thought of the penny. "That's generally the way it is in this world. Nothing seems to go right. I naturally thought I had found the beginning of my fortune, even if it was only a penny, and it turned out that the money belonged to somebody else. Oh dear!"

Well, the old rabbit traveler actually felt so badly that he didn't much care whether he found his fortune or not, and that is a very poor way to feel in this world, for one must never give up trying, no matter what happens.

Then Uncle Wiggily looked in his satchel to see if he had anything to eat, but my goodness sakes alive and a ham sandwich! There wasn't a thing in the valise! You see he was thinking so much about the penny that he forgot to put up his lunch.

"Humph! This is a pretty state of affairs!" exclaimed the old rabbit gentleman. "Worse and worse, and some more besides! I do declare! Hum! Suz! Dud!"

Well, he didn't know what to do, so he sat down on a log beside a shady bush and thought it all over. And the more he thought the sadder he became, until he began to believe he was the most miserable rabbit in all the world.

"Oh, dear! Oh, dear!" exclaimed Uncle Wiggily. "I might as well go back home and done with it."

But no sooner had he said this, than Uncle Wiggily heard the jolliest laugh he had ever known. Oh! it was such a rippling, happy joyous laugh that it would almost cure the toothache just to listen to it.

"Ha! Ha! Ho! Ho! He! He!" laughed the voice, and Uncle Wiggily looked up, and he looked down, and then he looked sideways and around a corner, but he could see no one. Still the laugh kept up, more jolly than ever.

"Humph! I wonder who that is?" said the rabbit. "I wish I could laugh like that," and Uncle Wiggily actually smiled the least little bit, and he didn't feel quite so sad.

Then, all at once, there was a voice singing, and this is the song, and if you feel sad when you sing it, just get some one to tickle you, or watch baby's face when he smiles, and you will feel jolly enough to sing this song, even if you have been crying because you stubbed your toe.

"Ha! Ha! Ho! Ho! I gladly sing,
I sing about most anything.
I sing about a pussy cat,
Who caught a little mousie-rat.
I sing about a doggie-dog,
Who saw a turtle on a log.
I sing about a little boy,
Who cried because he broke his toy.
And then he laughed, 'Ha! Ha! He! He!'

Howard R. Garis

Because he couldn't help it; see?"

"Well, well!" exclaimed Uncle Wiggily, "I wish I knew who that was. Perhaps it is a fairy, and if it is, I'm going to ask her for my fortune. I'm getting tired of not finding it," and when he thought about that he was sad again.

But a moment later a little black creature hopped out from under a leaf, and who should it be but a cricket.

"Was that you laughing?" asked the old gentleman rabbit, as he again looked in his valise to see if he had any sandwiches there. "Was it you?"

"It was," said the cricket. "I was just going - Oh, kindly excuse me, while I laugh again!" the cricket said, and then he laughed more jolly than before.

"What makes you so good-natured?" asked the rabbit.

"I just can't help it," said the cricket. "Everything is so lovely. The sun shines, and the birds sing, and the water in the brooks babble such jolly songs, and well - Oh, excuse me again if you please, I'm going to laugh once more," and so he did then and there. He just laughed and laughed and laughed, that cricket did.

"Well," said Uncle Wiggily, still speaking sadly, "of course it's nice to be jolly, anybody can be that way when the sun shines, but what about the rain? There! I guess you can't be jolly when it rains."

"Oh! when it rains I laugh because I know it will soon clear off, and then, too, I can think about the days when the sun did shine," said the cricket.

"Well," spoke Uncle Wiggily, "there is something in that, to be sure. And as you are such a jolly chap, will you travel along with me? Perhaps with you I could find my fortune."

"Of course I'll come," said the cricket, and he laughed again, and then he and the old gentleman rabbit hopped on together and Uncle Wiggily kept feeling more and more happy until he had forgotten all about the chipmunk's penny that wasn't his.

Well, in a little while, not so very long, the rabbit and the cricket came to a dark place in the woods. Oh! it was quite dismal, and, just as they passed a big, black stump with a hole in it, all of a sudden out popped the skillery-scalery-tailery alligator.

"Ah, ha!" exclaimed the unpleasant creature. "Now I have you both. I'm going to eat you both, first you, Mr. Cricket, and then you, Uncle Wiggily."

"Oh, please don't," begged the rabbit. "I haven't found my fortune yet."

"No matter," cried the alligator, "here we go!"

He made a grab for the cricket, but the little black insect hopped to one side, and then, all of a sudden he began to laugh. Oh, how hard he laughed.

"Ha! Ha! Ho! Ho! He! He!" My, it was wonderful! At first the alligator didn't know what to make of it. Harder and harder did the black cricket laugh, and then Uncle Wiggily began. He just couldn't help it. Harder and harder laughed the cricket and Uncle Wiggily together, and then, all at once, the alligator began to laugh. He couldn't help it either.

"Ha! Ha! Ho! Ho! He! He!" laughed the 'gator, and great big alligator tears rolled down his scaly cheeks, he laughed so hard. Why, he giggled so that he couldn't even have eaten a mosquito with mustard on.

"Come on, now!" suddenly cried the cricket to Uncle Wiggily. "Now is our chance to get away."

And before the alligator had stopped laughing they both hopped away in the woods together, and so the bad scalery-ailery-tailery creature didn't get either of them.

"My! it's a good thing you made him laugh," said the rabbit when they were safely away.

"It's a good thing to make anybody laugh," said the black cricket, and then he and Uncle Wiggily went on to seek the old gentleman rabbit's fortune.

And in the next story, in case the sunshine doesn't make my pussy cat sneeze and spill his milk, on the new door mat, I'll tell you all about Uncle Wiggily and the busy bug.

STORY XI

UNCLE WIGGILY AND THE BUSY BUG

Everywhere Uncle Wiggily and the black cricket went in the next few days, every one was glad to see them. For they were both so jolly, and laughed and joked so much along the road, that no one who heard them could be sad.

They came to one place where there was a boy sick with the toothache, and his mamma had done everything for him that she could think of, even to putting mustard on it, but still that boy's tooth ached.

Well, as soon as that boy saw the cricket and the old gentleman rabbit, and heard them laugh, why the boy smiled, and then the pain, somehow, seemed to be better, and he smiled some more, and then he laughed.

Then Uncle Wiggily told a funny story about a monkey who made faces at himself in a looking-glass, and got so excited about it that he jumped around behind the glass, thinking another monkey was there, and there wasn't, and the monkey fell into the freezer full of ice cream and caught cold because he ate so much of it.

Well, that boy opened his mouth real wide to laugh at the funny story and his mamma all of a sudden slipped a string around the aching tooth and she pulled it out in a moment, and it never ached again.

Howard R. Garis

"Oh, how glad I am!" cried the little boy. "I wish you would always stay with me, Uncle Wiggily - you and the jolly cricket."

"I'd like to, but I can't," said the old gentleman rabbit. "I must keep on after my fortune."

"I'll stay with you for a little while," said the cricket, and he did, telling some funny stories to other boys who had the toothache, and right away after that they allowed their bad teeth to be pulled, and their pain was over.

So Uncle Wiggily said good-by to the cricket and went on by himself. He was feeling very good now, for he and the cricket had met a kind muskrat, a thirty-fifth cousin to Nurse Jane Fuzzy-Wuzzy, and this muskrat gave Uncle Wiggily a lot of sandwiches for his satchel, so he wouldn't be hungry again for some time.

"And I don't mind so much about the cent, either," thought the rabbit, as he remembered the one that belonged to the chipmunk. "After all a cent is not so much, and I need more than that for my fortune. Ha! Ha! Ho! Ho!"

He just had to laugh, you see, when he thought of the jolly cricket. So he traveled on and on, over hill and dale, until one evening, just as the sun was going down behind the clouds, all red and golden and violet colored, he saw a little house built of green leaves.

"Ha!" exclaimed Uncle Wiggily. "That is a very fine house. I wish I had one like it in which to stay to-night. But it's too small for me. I guess I'll have to keep on and look for a haystack under which to crawl."

Well, just as he said that, all of a sudden there was a little rustling, scratching noise, and a bug came to the door of the queer little green leaf house. The bug had a broom and she began sweeping off the front porch and then she knocked the dirt out of the doormat, and then she swept some cobwebs off the shutters and then she hurried out and swept off the sidewalk, all so quickly that you could scarcely see her move.

"My, but she is a fast worker," said Uncle Wiggily. "She is almost as quick as Jennie Chipmunk."

"I have to be!" exclaimed the bug, for the old gentleman rabbit had spoken out loud without thinking, and the bug had heard him. "I have to hustle around," she said, "for I am the busy bug, and I have to keep busy. I work from morning to night to keep my house in order. Now excuse me; I have to go in and dust the piano," and she was just going to run in the house, when Uncle Wiggily said:

"Do you happen to know of a place where I can stay to-night?"

"Why, yes," said the busy bug. "Next door is a house where Mr. Groundhog used to live. But now he is away on his vacation, and I have the keys. I'm sure he wouldn't mind you staying in there over night. I'll get it in order for you. Come along, hurry up, no time to lose!"

And before Uncle Wiggily knew what was happening the busy bug had run in, got the keys, opened the front door of the groundhog's house. Then she flew in, and she began dusting it. My! what a dust she raised. Uncle Wiggily had to sneeze, there was so much of it.

And the funny part of it was that the house was already just as neat and clean as a piece of cocoanut or custard, or maybe even apple pie.

"Don't fuss any more with it," said Uncle Wiggily. "It will do very well as it is."

"Oh, it must be made cleaner," said the busy bug, and she swept and dusted until Uncle Wiggily sneezed again. Then the bug dusted a little more, and at last she said the house was in pretty fair shape and Uncle Wiggily could sleep there.

Then the busy bug flew back home and she kept busy up to nine o'clock, making beds and dusting the crumbs off the mantelpiece and picking up grains of sand off the floor. Then she went to sleep.

Well, along in the middle of the night Uncle Wiggily was awakened by hearing some one talking under his window. He looked out, and there were two savage old owls.

"Now, we'll fly right in through her window," said one owl, "and we'll eat her all up, and then we'll tear her house down."

And, would you believe it, they started right toward the house of the poor busy lady bug, who was fast asleep.

"Ha! This must never be!" cried Uncle Wiggily. "I must save her. How can I do it?" So he looked around, and he saw a broom, which the busy bug had left behind when she finished sweeping. "That will do!" cried the rabbit. He took it in his paws and, leaning out of the window, he held it just as if it was a gun, and cried:

"Now, you bad owls, fly away or I'll shoot all your feathers off! Fly away and don't you harm my friend, the busy lady bug!"

Well, sir, those owls were so frightened, thinking that Uncle Wiggily was going to shoot them with the broom-gun (only, of course, they didn't know it was only a broom), and, would you believe it, they were terribly afraid and they flew off into the dark woods, and so didn't eat up the busy bug after all, and she slept in peace and quietness, never even waking up, she was so tired after being busy all day.

Then Uncle Wiggily went back to bed, and the owls didn't disturb him again that night. And in the morning the busy bug got his breakfast and thanked him when he told her about scaring the owls away with the make-believe broom-gun.

Uncle Wiggily traveled on, and soon he had another adventure. What it was I'll tell you almost right away, when, in case the cake of ice doesn't melt, and make a mud puddle for the baby to fall into, I'll tell you about Uncle Wiggily and the funny monkey.

STORY XII

UNCLE WIGGILY AND THE FUNNY MONKEY

It was a bright and beautiful sunshiny day, and Uncle Wiggily was hopping along the road, thinking many thoughts and about the busy bug and the black cricket and all things like that and how hard it was to look and look for your fortune and never find it, when all of a sudden, just as he happened to put his crutch down on a round stone, it slipped, and down he fell kerthump.

"Oh, wow! Ouch!" cried the old gentleman rabbit as he bumped his nose on a sharp stick. "That hurt! My, I hope I haven't broken one of my ears or paw-nails. If I did I'll have to get in the ambulance and go to the hospital."

So he sat up very slowly and carefully and looked himself all over and he was glad to see that he hadn't broken anything except a lettuce sandwich that he carried in his satchel and, as it was just as good broken as it was whole, it didn't matter much.

"Oh, are you hurt?" suddenly cried a voice, as Uncle Wiggily took some dirt out of his left ear. "If you are I can give you something to put on your cuts," and out from under a big leaf came a beautiful butterfly.

"What can you put on my cuts?" asked the rabbit.

"Oh, I can get some sticky gum from a tree or a flower and spread it on a leaf and make some court plaster," spoke the butterfly. "It will cure a cut very quickly."

"Thank you very much," said Uncle Wiggily, "but very luckily I haven't any cuts. I'm all right, I guess, but because you are so kind to me here is just a drop of honey that I found in the bottom of my satchel. The bee gave it to me." So he handed to the kind butterfly a little honey he had left. The butterfly was very glad to get it, and fluttered away, jumping from one flower to another as easily as a boy can spin his top.

Then the old gentleman rabbit traveled on, and pretty soon, when it was just about time for dinner, he came to a beautiful place in the woods. The trees were nice and green and shady, and there was a little brook that was bubbling and babbling over the mossy stones and then all at once Uncle Wiggily heard the queerest music he had ever heard. It was like forty-'leven bands all playing in the park at once.

"My, I must be near a big picnic!" cried the rabbit. "I shall have to look out for myself, or some boys may chase me."

The music kept getting louder but still the old gentleman rabbit didn't see any people, and he went on very slowly until he came to a little house built of shingles, and there in front of it sat a monkey. And he was the funniest monkey you ever saw.

For that monkey was playing five hand organs all at once. Yes, just as true as I'm telling you, he was. He played one organ with his left paw and he played another organ with his right paw, and he played still another with his left foot and he twisted the crank of another with his right foot. And then, to finish off with, he whirled around the crank of the fifth organ with his long tail. Oh, he was a smart monkey, I tell you!

"My! This is almost as good as a circus!" exclaimed Uncle Wiggily. "I'm glad I came this way."

Howard R. Garis

Well, that funny monkey played faster than ever, and on one organ he played the tune "Please Bring Your Umbrella Inside When it Rains," and on another he played "May I Have Some of Your Ice Cream Cone if I Give You a Kiss?" And on the third hand organ the monkey was playing the tune "Come Out Into the Hammock and See Who'll Fall Out First," and another tune was "Please Don't Let that Big Black Bug Tickle Me," and on the organ that he twisted with his tail the monkey ground out the song "Come On Inside the Motorboat and Have a Nice, Cool Swim."

"My, how do you do it?" asked the rabbit of the monkey. "You must be very musical."

"Oh, it comes natural to me," said the monkey, not a bit proud like.

"But where did you get so many organs?"

"Oh, I saved up my pennies for them," said the monkey. "You see, it was this way. I used to work for a man who had a hand organ, and he used to take me around with him to climb up on the porches, and in the second-story windows to get the pennies from the children. Well, I always loved music, and I wanted the man to let me play his organ, but he never would. So I made up my mind I would save up all my pennies and some day buy an organ for myself.

"Well, I did that, for you know often when I used to go around to collect pennies for the man, some children would give me a few for myself. Finally I got rich and I didn't work for the man any longer, and I had enough to buy five hand organs, for I can play five at once. Then I came here, and built this shingle house and every day I amuse myself by playing tunes, and I never have to climb up the rainwater pipe to get money. Oh, it is a happy life," and the monkey felt so funny that he hung by his tail from a tree branch, and made faces at Uncle Wiggily - just in fun, you understand.

Uncle Wiggily was very glad he had met the monkey, and he listened to the music, and the monkey even let the rabbit play one tune for himself, and it was called, "When You Wiggle Your Wiggily Ears Wiggle Them Good and Hard."

And then, all of a sudden, just as that tune was finished, there was a terrible noise in the bushes.

"My goodness! What's that?" cried the monkey as he hopped up on top of one of his hand organs and curled his tail around the handle.

"It sounds like a bear!" said the rabbit. "But don't worry. I'll do just as the cricket did to the alligator and make him laugh so that he won't hurt us."

"Good!" cried the monkey. And then the noise became louder and out from the bushes popped a big animal. But it was an elephant instead of a bear, and as soon as he saw the monkey and Uncle Wiggily he ran up to them and shook his trunk at them and cried:

"Oh, I'm so glad to see you! I just got away from the circus, and I want to have some fun!" and he was as kind and gentle as he could be and he and Uncle Wiggily had quite an adventure the next day.

I'll tell you about it on the next page, when, in case the little boy across the street doesn't tickle my pussy cat and make him sneeze the rubbers off the umbrella plant, the story will be about Uncle Wiggily and the big dog.

Howard R. Garis

STORY XIII

UNCLE WIGGILY AND THE BIG DOG

Let's see, I left off in the last story just where the elephant came out of the woods and shook his tail - I mean his trunk - at Uncle Wiggily and the funny monkey, didn't I? Well, now, I'm going to tell you what happened after that.

"Why did you run away from the circus?" asked the old gentleman rabbit of the elephant. "I should think you would like it there. I know Sammie and Susie Littletail would love a circus."

"Yes, some folks like it," spoke the elephant slow and thoughtful-like, as he sat down on his trunk, "but I do not care for it. You see of late the children ate all the peanuts, instead of giving me my share, and I just couldn't stand it any longer. Why, it got so, finally, that when a man would give his little boy five cents to buy a bag of peanuts for me the little boy would eat all but two or three of the nuts, and those were all he gave to me. It wasn't enough, so I ran away."

"I don't in the least blame you," said the monkey, "and I'm going to let you play some of my hand organs."

Well, the elephant was delighted at that, and he played one organ with his trunk and another one with his tail, making some very nice music.

Uncle Wiggily stayed in the monkey's house that night, and the elephant wanted to come in also, but of course he was far too big, so he had to sleep outside under a tree. It was an apple tree, and in the middle of the night the elephant snored so hard and heavily through his trunk that he shook the tree and all the apples fell off, and in the morning the monkey made an apple pie from some of them.

"I think I had better start off on my travels again," said the old gentleman rabbit after breakfast. "There must be a fortune for me somewhere if I can only find it. So I'll trot along."

"I'll go with you," said the kind elephant. "Perhaps you might see your fortune in the top of a tall tree, and then you couldn't get it. But I would pull the tree down for you."

"That would be fine!" cried Uncle Wiggily. "I'll be glad to have you travel with me."

So they said good-by to the monkey, and off they started together, the rabbit and the elephant. They talked of many things, about how hot it was, and whether there would be rain soon, and about how much ice cream cones cost, and sometimes what a little bit of ice cream the man puts in the cones when he is in a hurry.

"Speaking of ice cream cones," said the elephant, "makes me hungry for some. I wish I had one."

"I wish I had one also," spoke Uncle Wiggily. "You would have to have a very large one, though, Mr. Elephant, but a small one would do for me."

"Don't say another word," cried the elephant as he waved his trunk in the air. "I'm going right off and get us some ice cream cones. I know where there's a store. You hop along slowly and I'll catch up to you."

So the elephant went off to the ice cream cone store, and

Uncle Wiggily, with his valise and the barber pole crutch, hopped on through the woods, looking about to see if his fortune was up in any of the trees, but it wasn't there yet.

Well, pretty soon, in a little while, not so very long, all of a sudden the old gentleman rabbit heard a sniffing-sniffing noise in the woods. And then there was a rustling in the bushes.

"Ha, hum!" exclaimed the rabbit. "Perhaps that may be a bear. I had better look out for myself."

He started to hop softly away, so the bear, or whatever it was, wouldn't hear him, but he was too late. In an instant out of the bushes popped something big and black and shaggy, and the rabbit, taking one look at it, saw that it was a big dog.

"New is the time for me to run!" cried Uncle Wiggily. "That dog will eat me up, sure pop!"

Away hopped the old gentleman rabbit, his heart going "pitter-patter-pat," he was so frightened. On and on he ran down a path in the woods.

"Here, come back here! Come back!" cried the dog.

"Indeed, I will not," answered Uncle Wiggily. "I know what you want to do. You want to eat me."

"No, I don't, honestly!" cried the dog. "But come back, for if you run any farther on that road you'll fall into a lake and be drowned."

"Humph! I don't believe that!" cried the rabbit. "You are saying that to scare me," and on he hopped faster than ever.

"Come back! Come back!" cried the dog again, but Uncle Wiggily wouldn't. My! how fast he did hop, until, all of a sudden, as he returned around the corner of a stump, he saw a lake of water right in front of him. And before he could stop himself he had fallen plump into it; crutch, satchel and all, and of course he couldn't swim. And he could hear the dog coming barking down the path after him.

"Oh, this is the end of me, sure pop!" thought poor Uncle Wiggily. "I'll never get any fortune now."

"Oh, dear!" cried the dog. "I told you how it would be. I tried to save you from getting in the water," and then the rabbit knew the big dog had been telling the truth. But it was too late now. Uncle Wiggily was going down under the deep, dark, cold water when, all of a sudden, along came the elephant with a great big ice cream cone for himself, and a little one for Uncle Wiggily. He saw the rabbit in the water and he also saw the big shaggy dog.

"Did you push Uncle Wiggily in the water?" asked the elephant, "because if you did I'm going to throw you in."

"No, indeed, I didn't," answered the dog. "It was an accident," and he told the elephant how it happened. "But I'll jump in, grab him and swim out with him," said the dog.

"No, don't do that, you might accidentally bite him," spoke the elephant. "I have a better plan." So he laid down the ice cream cones and then he put the end of his hollow trunk in the lake, and he began to suck up and drink the water, just as you suck lemonade up through a straw.

And presto chango! in a few seconds all the water was sucked out of the lake by the elephant, and it was dry land and the rabbit could walk safely to shore, and so he wasn't drowned after all. And how he did thank the elephant! Uncle Wiggily ate his ice cream cone, and the elephant gave some of his to the dog, and they were all happy.

Now, if the elephant doesn't get a sliver in his foot so he can't dance at the hoptoads' picnic, I'll tell you in the next story about Uncle Wiggily and the peanut man.

Howard R. Garis

STORY XIV

UNCLE WIGGILY AND THE PEANUT MAN

After Uncle Wiggily and the elephant and the big dog had eaten up the ice cream cones, they sat in the woods a while and looked at the place where the watery lake had been before the elephant drank it up to save the rabbit from drowning.

"My, but you must be strong to take up all that water," said the dog.

"Yes, I guess I am pretty strong," said the elephant, though he was not at all proud-like. "I will show you how I can pull up a tree," he said. So he wound his trunk around a big tree and he gave one great, heaving pull and up that tree came by the roots. Then, all of a sudden a voice cried:

"Oh, you're upsetting all my eggs!" and a robin, who had her nest in the tree, fluttered around feeling very sad.

"Oh, excuse me, Mrs. Robin," said the elephant. "I would not have disturbed you for the world had I known that your nest was in that tree. I'll plant it right back again in the same place I pulled it up. Anyhow, I intended to do it, as it is not a good thing to kill a tree. I'll plant it again."

So he put the tree back in the hole, and with his big feet he stamped down the earth around it. Then the robin's nest and eggs were safe, and she sang a pretty song because she was thankful to the elephant.

Well, the elephant had to sleep out-of-doors again that night, because he couldn't find a house large enough for him, but Uncle Wiggily slept in the big dog's kennel. In the morning the rabbit said:

"It is very nice here, and I like it very much, but I must travel along, I s'pose, and see if I can't find my fortune. Are you coming, Mr. Elephant?"

"Why, certainly. I will go along with you," said the big chap. "Perhaps the dog will come also."

"No, thank you," said the dog. "I am going to meet a friend of mine, named Percival, and we are going to call on Lulu and Alice and Jimmie Wibblewobble, the duck children."

"Is that so?" exclaimed Uncle Wiggily. "Why, Percival and the Wibblewobbles are friends of mine. Kindly give them my love and say that I hope soon to get back home with my fortune."

So the dog said he would, and he started off to meet Percival, who used to work in the same circus where the elephant came from. And the rabbit and the elephant hurried off together down the road.

"Are you ever going back to the circus?" asked Uncle Wiggily of the elephant as they went along.

"Not unless they catch me and make me go," he answered. "I like this sort of life much better, and besides, no one gave me ice cream cones in the circus."

Well, pretty soon the rabbit and the elephant came to a place where there was a high mountain.

"Oh, we'll never get up that," said Uncle Wiggily.

Howard R. Garis

"Yes, we will," said the elephant, "I'll make a hole through it with my tusks, and we can walk under it instead of climbing over."

So with his long, sharp tusks he made a tunnel right through the mountain, and, though it was a bit darkish, he and the rabbit went through it as easily as a mouse can nibble a bit of cheese.

Then, a little later they came to a place where there was a big river to cross, and there was no bridge.

"Oh, we can never get over that," said Uncle Wiggily.

"Yes, we can," said the elephant.

"Are you going to drink it up as you did the lake?" asked the rabbit.

"No," said the elephant, "but I will make a bridge to go over the river." So he found a great big tree that the wind had blown down, and, taking this in his strong trunk, the elephant laid it across the river, and then he laid another tree and another, and pretty soon he had as good a bridge as one could wish, and he and Uncle Wiggily crossed over on it.

Well, they hadn't gone on very far, before, all of a sudden the elephant fell down, and he was so heavy that he shook the ground just like when a locomotive choo-choo engine rushes past.

"Oh, whatever is the matter?" asked Uncle Wiggily. "Did you hurt yourself?"

"No," said the elephant, sad-like, "I am not hurt, but I am sick. I guess I drank too much ice water, which is a bad thing to do in hot weather. Oh, how ill I am! You had better go for a doctor."

Well, that poor elephant was so ill that he had to lie down on the ground, and he cried and groaned, and the big tears rolled down his trunk, and made quite a mud puddle on the earth. For when an elephant is ill he is very ill, indeed, as there is so much of him.

"I'll cover you with leaves so you won't get sunburned," said Uncle Wiggily, "and then I'll hop off for a doctor." Well, it takes a great number of leaves to cover up an elephant, but finally the rabbit did it, and then away he started.

He looked everywhere for an elephant doctor, but he couldn't seem to find any. There were dog doctors and horse doctors and cat doctors and even doctors for boys and girls, but none for the elephant.

"Oh, what shall I do?" thought the rabbit. "My poor, dear elephant may die."

Just then he heard some one singing in the woods like this:

"Peanuts, they are good to eat,
Mine are most especially neat,
I am going to make them hot
So that you will eat a lot."

"Oh, are you an elephant doctor?" cried Uncle Wiggily.

"No, I am a hot-peanut-man," said the voice, and then the peanut roaster began to whistle like a tea-kettle. "But, perhaps I can cure a sick elephant," said the peanut man. So he and Uncle Wiggily hurried off through the woods to where the elephant was groaning, and, would you believe it? as soon as the big chap heard the whistle of the hot-peanut wagon and smelled the nuts roasting he got well all of a sudden and he ate a bushel of the nuts and Uncle Wiggily had some also. So that's how the elephant got well, and he and the rabbit traveled on the next day.

Howard R. Garis

They had quite an adventure, too, as I shall have the pleasure of telling you in the next story which will be about Uncle Wiggily and the crawly snake - that is if the baby doesn't drop his bread and butter down the stovepipe and make the rice pudding laugh.

STORY XV

UNCLE WIGGILY AND THE CRAWLY SNAKE

"Do you feel all right to travel to-day?" asked Uncle Wiggily of the elephant the next morning, after the hot-peanut-man had cured the big chap.

"Oh, yes, I feel very fine!" said the elephant. "We will travel along together again, and perhaps we may find your fortune this time."

"Hadn't we better take some extra peanuts with us, in case you become ill again?" asked the rabbit, as he looked in the satchel to see if he had any sandwiches, in case he got hungry.

"Oh, to be sure, we must have peanuts!" exclaimed the elephant. "Take as many as we can carry, for I just love 'em!"

So they hunted up the hot-peanut-man, and bought all the rest of his peanuts, besides paying for those the elephant had eaten to make himself get well.

"Good luck to you!" cried the peanut man, as he wheeled away his empty wagon, "I wish I had elephants for customers every day, then I would soon get rich," and away he went singing:

"I sell peanuts good and hot,
Five cents buys you quite a lot.
Get your money and come here,

Howard R. Garis

Buy my peanuts, children dear.

"My peanuts are hot and brown,
Finest ones in all the town.
Nice and juicy - good to chew,
I have some for all of you."

"Well, come on," said the elephant to Uncle Wiggily, "put some peanuts in your valise, and I will carry the rest."

"How; in your trunk?" asked the rabbit.

"No, I'm going to wrap them up in a bundle, and tie them on my back. I want my trunk to squirt water through when it gets hot, as I think the sun is going to be very scorchy to-day."

So he tied the bundle of peanuts on his back, and then the two friends journeyed on together. Well, it did get very hot, and it kept on getting hotter, and there wasn't much shade.

"Oh my, I wish it would rain a little shower!" said Uncle Wiggily, as he wiped his ears with his handkerchief. "I am as hot as an oven."

"I can soon fix that part of it," said the elephant. And pretty soon he came to a spring of cold water, and he sucked a lot of it up in his hollow trunk, and then he squirted a nice cool, fine spray of it over the rabbit, just as if it came out of a hose with which papa waters the garden or lawn.

"My! That feels fine!" said the rabbit. Then the elephant squirted some water on himself, and they went on, feeling much better.

But still they were warm again in a short time, and then the elephant said:

"I know what I am going to do. I am going to get some more ice cream cones. They will cool us off better than anything else. I'll go for them and bring back some big ones. You stay here in the shade, Uncle Wiggily, but don't walk on ahead, or you may tumble into the water again."

"I'll not," promised the rabbit. "I'll wait right here for you."

Off the elephant started to get the ice cream cones and pretty soon he came to the store where the man sold them.

"I want two of your very coldest cones," said the elephant to the man, for sometimes, in stories, you know, elephants can talk to people. "I want a big strawberry cone for myself," the elephant went on, "and a smaller one for my friend, Uncle Wiggily, the rabbit."

"Very well," said the man, "but you will have to wait until I make a large cone for you."

So that man took seventeen thousand, six hundred and eighty-seven little cones and made them into one big one for the elephant. Then he took eighteen thousand, two hundred and ninety-one quarts of strawberry ice cream, and an extra pint, and put it into the big cone. Then he made a rabbit-sized ice cream cone for Uncle Wiggily and gave them both to the elephant, who carried them in his trunk so they wouldn't melt.

But I must tell you what was happening to Uncle Wiggily all this while. As he sat there in the shade of the apple tree, thinking, about his fortune and whether he would ever find it, all of a sudden he saw something round and squirming sticking itself toward him through the bushes.

"Ha! the elephant has come back so quietly that I didn't hear him," thought the rabbit. "That is his trunk he is sticking out at me. I guess he thinks I don't see him, and he is going to tickle me. I hope he has those ice cream cones."

Well, the crawly, squirming, round thing, which was like the small end of an elephant's trunk, kept coming closer and closer to the rabbit.

"Now, I'll play a trick on that elephant - I'll tickle his trunk for him, and he'll think it's a mosquito!" said Uncle Wiggily to himself.

He was just about to do this, when suddenly the crawly thing made a sort of jump toward him, and before the rabbit could move he found himself grasped by a big, ugly snake, who wrapped himself around the rabbit just as ladies wrap their fur around their necks in the winter. It wasn't the elephant's trunk at all, but a bad snake.

"Now, I have you!" hissed the snake like a steam radiator in Uncle Wiggily's left ear. "I'm going to squeeze you to death and then eat you," and he began to squeeze that poor rabbit just like the wash-lady squeezes clothes in the wringer.

"Oh, my breath! You are crushing all the breath out of me!" cried Uncle Wiggily. "Please let go of me!"

"No!" hissed the snake, and he squeezed harder than ever.

"Oh, this is the end of me!" gasped the rabbit, when all of a sudden he heard a great crashing in the bushes. Then a voice cried:

"Here, you bad snake, let go of Uncle Wiggily."

And bless my hat! If the elephant didn't rush up, just in time, and he grabbed hold of that snake's tail in his trunk, and unwound the snake from around the rabbit, and then the elephant with a long swing of his trunk threw the snake so high up in the air that I guess he hasn't yet come down.

"I was just in time to save you!" said the elephant to Uncle Wiggily. "Here, eat this ice cream cone and you'll feel better."

So the rabbit did this, and his breath came back and he was all right again, but he made up his mind never to try to tickle a crawly thing again until he was sure it wasn't a snake.

So that's all for the present, if you please, but in case my fur hat doesn't sleep out in the hammock all night, and catch cold in the head so that it sneezes and wakes up the alarm clock, I'll tell you next about Uncle Wiggily and the water lilies.

Howard R. Garis

STORY XVI

UNCLE WIGGILY AND THE WATER LILIES

Uncle Wiggily was hopping along through the woods one day, and pretty soon, as he went past a cute little house, made out of corncobs, he heard some one calling to him.

"Oh, Mr. Rabbit," a voice said, "have you seen anything of my little girl?" And there stood a nice mamma cat, looking anxiously about.

"I don't know," answered Uncle Wiggily, as he stopped in the shade of a tree, and set down his valise. "Was your little girl named Sarah, Mrs. Cat?"

"Oh, indeed, my little girl is not named Sarah," said Mrs. Cat. "She is called Snowball, and she is just as cute as she can be. She is all white, like a ball of snow, and so we call her Snowball. But she is lost, and I'm afraid I'll never find her again," and the kittie's mamma began to cry, and she wiped her tears on her apron.

"Oh, don't worry. Never mind. I'll find her for you," said the kind old gentleman rabbit.

"I can't find my fortune but I believe I can find Snowball. Now, tell me which way she went away, and I'll go search for her."

"I didn't see her go out of the house," said Mrs. Cat, "because I was making a cherry pie, and I was very busy. Snowball was playing on the floor, with a ball of soft yarn, and it rolled out of doors. She raced out after it, and I thought she would soon be back. I put the cherry pie in the oven and then when I went to look for her she was gone. Oh, dear! I just know some horrid dog has hurt her."

"Please don't worry," said Uncle Wiggily. "I'll find her for you. I'll start right off, and if I can't find her I'll get a policeman, and he can, for the police always find lost children."

So Uncle Wiggily started off, leaving his valise with Mrs. Cat, but taking his crutch with him, for he thought he might need it to beat off any bad dogs if they chased after Snowball.

First the old gentleman rabbit looked carefully all along the road, but he couldn't see anything of the lost pussy cat.

"Perhaps she may be up a tree," he said to himself. "If a dog chased her she would climb up one, and perhaps she is afraid to come down."

So he looked up into all the trees, and he even shook some of them in order to see up them better, but he did not discover the pussy cat. Then he called:

"Snowball! Snowball! Snowball! Where are you?"

But there was no answer.

"Oh, if there was only some bird who could call 'Snowball' I would get them to call for the lost pussy," thought Uncle Wiggily.

Then he looked up and he saw a big black bird sitting on a tree.

"Can you call 'Snowball' for me?" asked the rabbit, politely.

Howard R. Garis

"She is lost and her mamma wants her very much. Just call 'Snowball' as loudly as you can."

"I can't," said the big black bird. "All I can cry is 'Caw! Caw! Caw!' I am a crow, you see."

"That is too bad," said the rabbit. "Then I will have to keep on searching by myself," so he did, and the crow flew away to look for a cornfield that had no scarecrow in it to frighten him.

Well, Uncle Wiggily looked in all the places he could think of, but still there was no pussy to be seen, and he was just thinking he had better go for a policeman. But he thought he would try just one more place, so he looked down a hollow stump, but Snowball was not there.

"I'll have to get a policeman after all," said the rabbit, so he told a policeman cat about the lost pussy, and the policeman cat searched for Snowball, but he couldn't find her, either.

"I guess she is gone," said the policeman. "You had better go back and tell her mamma that she hasn't any little pussy girl any more."

"Oh, how sad it will be to do that!" cried Uncle Wiggily. "I just can't bear to."

But he started back to the corncob house to tell Mrs. Cat that he couldn't find her Snowball. And all the while he kept feeling more and more sad, until he was almost ready to cry.

"But I must be brave," said the old gentleman rabbit, and just then he came to a pond where a whole lot of beautiful, white water lilies were growing. Oh, they are a lovely flower, with such a sweet, spicy smell. As soon as Uncle Wiggily saw them he said:

"I'll pick some and take them home to Mrs. Cat. Perhaps they will make her feel a little happy, even if her Snowball is gone forever."

So with his long crutch Uncle Wiggily pulled toward shore some of the water lilies, until he could pick them on their slender stems. Some of the flowers were wide open, and some were closed, like rosebuds.

He took both kinds home to Mrs. Cat, and when he told her he couldn't find Snowball she was very sorrowful and she cried. But she loved the flowers very much, and put them in a bowl of water.

"I'll stay here to-night," said the rabbit, "and in the morning I'll look for Snowball again. I'm sure I'll find her."

"Oh, you are very kind," said Mrs. Cat, as she wiped away her tears.

Well, the next morning Uncle Wiggily got up real early, and the first thing he saw was the bowl of water lilies on the parlor table. They had all closed up like buds in the night, but in the sunlight they all opened again into beautiful flowers.

And, would you believe me, right in the middle of one of the flowers something white moved and wiggled. Then it gave a little "Mew!" and then Uncle Wiggily cried:

"Oh, Mrs. Cat, come here quickly! Here is Snowball! She was asleep inside of one of the water lilies!"

And, surely enough, there was the little lost kittie, just awakening in one of the flowers, and she was exactly the color of it. And, oh, how glad she was to see her mamma again, and how her mamma did hug her!

"How did you get in that flower?" asked Uncle Wiggily.

"Oh, when I went after my ball a big dog chased me," said Snowball, "so I jumped into one of the lilies and I fell asleep, and the flower went shut and I stayed there. But now I'm home, and I'm glad of it," and she just kissed Uncle Wiggily on the tip end of his nose, that twinkled like a star on a frosty night.

So that's how Snowball was lost and found, and I'm going to tell you about Uncle Wiggily and the sunflower, that is if the sunfish doesn't spread the butter too thick on the baby's bread with his tail and make her slide out of her high chair.

STORY XVII

UNCLE WIGGILY AND THE SUNFLOWER

Mrs. Cat and her daughter Snowball liked Uncle Wiggily so much that they wanted him to stay with them a long time.

"You can build yourself a nice little corncob house next to ours," said Snowball, "and live in it; and you can tell me a story every night."

"Oh, but rabbits live underground, and not in corncob houses, though such houses are very nice," said Uncle Wiggily. "I guess I'll have to be traveling on."

"If you stay, I'll bake you a cherry pie every day," said Mrs. Cat. "And you can help find Snowball when she gets lost again."

"Cherry pie is very good, and you are very kind," said the rabbit politely, "but I have my fortune to find."

"Well, if you can't stay you can't, I s'pose," said Snowball; "but I'm never going to get lost again," and she put her little nose down deep inside a water lily and smelled it, and oh, how sweet and spicy it smelled!

So Uncle Wiggily got ready to start off on his travels again, and in his satchel he put a whole cherry pie that Mrs. Cat had baked for him.

Howard R. Garis

"It will taste good when you are hungry," she said.

"Indeed it will," agreed Uncle Wiggily, and he wished he was hungry then and there, because he just loved cherry pie.

He was walking on through the woods, when, all at once, he heard some music playing, and the name of the song was "Never Take Your Ice Cream Cone and Drop it in the Mud."

"Ha! I believe that is the funny monkey and one of his hand organs!" exclaimed the rabbit. "I shall be glad to see him again."

So he looked through the trees, and there, surely enough, was the monkey, and he was playing the organ with his tail, and in one paw he held a cocoanut and in the other paw an orange, and first he would take a bite of the orange, and then a bite of the cocoanut.

"I always like music when I eat," said the monkey as he threw a bit of orange skin over his left shoulder.

"How comes it that you are away off here," asked the rabbit.

"Oh! I got tired of staying home," said the monkey. "I thought I would go out and see if I could make a few pennies by playing music." Then he played another tune called, "Don't Sit Down When You Stand Up."

Well, Uncle Wiggily listened to the music, which he liked very much, and he began to feel hungry. Then he thought of the cherry pie, that the cat lady had put in his valise.

"I guess I'll eat some of that and give the monkey a bit," he said, and he did so.

"Oh, this is most delicious and scrumptious!" cried the monkey, as he and Uncle Wiggily sat there eating the pie, and wiping off the juice with green leaves, so as not to soil their clothing.

"Indeed, it is very delectable," said the rabbit, hungry-like. "Have another piece."

Well, he was just cutting it off, when, all of a sudden, before you could say "Boo!" to an elephant, a terrible voice cried:

"Here! Give me that pie! I must have cherry pie!" and before the monkey or Uncle Wiggily knew what was happening, out from behind the bushes jumped the skillery-scallery-tailery alligator, gnashing his teeth.

"Give me that pie!" he cried again, opening his mouth wide enough to swallow a cake as big as a wash-tub.

"No, you cannot have it," said Uncle Wiggily, and, as quick as a wink, he popped the pie into his valise and closed it up. "Now you can't get it!" the rabbit said.

"Then I'll get you and the monkey!" cried the alligator, as he made a dash for both of them.

"Not me! You can't catch me!" exclaimed the monkey, as he skipped up into the top of a tall tree. Then, of course, as the alligator couldn't climb a tree he couldn't get the monkey. The skillery-scallery creature tried to eat the hand organ, and he tried to play it, but he could do neither. Then he got real angry.

"I'll chase after Uncle Wiggily and eat him!" he cried out, for by this time the rabbit was hopping along down the road. After him went the 'gator, coming nearer and nearer.

"Stop! Stop! I want you!" cried the alligator to the rabbit.

"I know you do, but you can't have me!" replied the rabbit. "I don't want to be eaten up!"

Howard R. Garis

So he ran on as fast as he could, but still the alligator came on after him, and the savage beast was almost up to Uncle Wiggily.

"Oh, if I only had some place to hide!" panted the poor rabbit. "Then maybe the alligator would pass me by."

So he looked around for a place in which to hide, but just then he found himself in a field, and all that he could see were a whole lot of sunflowers growing near a fence.

"Oh, I can't hide behind those flowers because the stems are so small around," thought Uncle Wiggily. "And I can't climb up them, and sit on the big flower, because I can't climb, and besides the stems are too slender to hold me up. Oh, what shall I do?"

Well, the alligator was coming nearer and nearer, and the rabbit could hear the gnashing of his teeth, when, all at once one of the sunflowers called out.

"Gnaw through my stem, and cut me down, Uncle Wiggily. Then you can hold my big blossom up in front of you and the alligator can't see you."

"But won't it hurt you to cut you down?" asked the rabbit.

"No, for I will grow up again next year," said the big sunflower. "Hurry and cut me down, and hide behind me, and I'll shine in the eyes of the alligator and blind him."

So Uncle Wiggily quickly gnawed through the sunflower stalk with his sharp teeth, and down the flower came. Then the rabbit held the blossom up in front of himself, and hid behind it, and the yellow flower, which is round, just like the sun, shone so brightly into the alligator's face that he couldn't look out of his eyes, and so he was partly blinded, and he couldn't see to catch Uncle Wiggily, and he had to crawl away without eating the rabbit.

Then Uncle Wiggily thanked the sunflower, and laid it gently down, and hopped on his way again to seek his fortune.

And the story after this, in case the washbowl and pitcher don't do a funny dance in the middle of the night and wake up my puppy dog, I'll tell you about Uncle Wiggily and the lightning bugs.

STORY XVIII

UNCLE WIGGILY AND THE LIGHTNING BUG

It was a very warm day, and as Uncle Wiggily walked along, carrying his satchel, and sort of leaning on his crutch, for his rheumatism hurt him a bit, he said:

"It is very hard to have to look for your fortune on a hot day, I wish it was nice and cool, and then I would feel better."

"I can tell you where there is a cool place," said a little yellow bird, as she flew along in the air over the head of the old gentleman rabbit.

"Do you mean in an icehouse?" asked the traveling rabbit as he took off his hat to see if the sun had burned it any.

"No, but of course that is a cold place," said the bird, as she sang a funny little song about a curly-headed dog who hadn't any nose and every time he walked along he stepped upon his toes. "But I don't mean an icehouse," went on the bird, as she turned her head to one side. "However, I know a nice cool place in the woods where you can lie down and have a little sleep. By that time the hot sun will go down behind the clouds, and then you can travel on in comfort."

"I believe that will be a good plan," spoke the rabbit. "I'll do it. Please show me the way to the cool place."

So the bird flew on ahead, and Uncle Wiggily hopped on behind, and pretty soon he came to a place in the woods where there was a little babbling brook, flowing over mossy green stones, and telling them secrets about the fishes that swam in the cool water. Then there were long, green ferns leaning over, and nodding their heads as they dipped down to take a drink out of the brook. There was also a nice little cave, made of stones, and that was almost as cool as an icehouse.

"Oh, this will be just fine for me!" exclaimed the rabbit, as he hopped inside the stone cave. "I'll go to sleep here."

So he stretched out on a pile of leaves, and the little yellow bird began to sing a sleepy song. This is how it went, to the tune "Lum-tum-tum tiddily-iddily-um:"

"Sleep, Uncle Wiggily, sleep.
Don't open your eyes to peep.
I'll sing you a song,
That's not very long.
It's not sad, so please do not weep."

Well, as true as I'm telling you, before she had sung more than forty-'leven verses the old gentleman rabbit was fast, fast asleep, and, no matter how hot the sun shone down, Uncle Wiggily was nice and cool.

Well, pretty soon, in a little while, a savage, bad hawk-bird flew down from high in the air, where he had seen the little yellow bird sitting on the tree, near the cave, where the rabbit was sleeping. And the hawk made a dash for the yellow bird, and would have eaten her up only the bird flew quickly away and hid in a hollow stump, and that hawk was so mad that he bit a leaf off a tree and tore it into three pieces - the leaf, I mean, not the tree.

Well, after that the yellow bird didn't dare stay near the cave, for the hawk was on the watch to catch her, and, of course, Uncle Wiggily had no one to awaken him when it was cool

Howard R. Garis

enough for him to travel on and seek his fortune.

He slept and he slept, and then he slept a little more, and all of a sudden he awakened and it was nearly night. My! how he did jump up then and rub his eyes with his paws, and he couldn't think, for a minute or so, just where he was.

"Oh, now I remember!" he exclaimed. "I'm in the cave. Oh, dear me! but it's coming on night. The yellow bird must have forgotten to wake me up. I wonder what I shall do?"

So he went out of the cave to look for the bird, but he couldn't find her. The savage hawk was there, however, but when he saw Uncle Wiggily and noted how brave he was, even if he did have the rheumatism, that hawk just gnashed his beak and flew away.

Then it got darker and darker, and poor Uncle Wiggily didn't know what to do, for he didn't know whether or not it would be safe to stay in the cave.

"A bear might come along and eat me," he thought. "This cave might be a bear's den. I guess I will travel ahead and look for some other place where I can spend the night. But I don't like traveling in the dark."

However, there was no help for it, so the old gentleman rabbit, after eating a lettuce sandwich, took up his satchel, grasped his crutch firmly, and started away.

He traveled on through the woods, and it kept getting darker and darker, until at last Uncle Wiggily couldn't see anything in front of him but just blackness.

"Oh, this will never do!" he cried. "I can't go on this way. If I only had a lantern it would be all right."

Then, all at once, he heard a sort of growling noise in the bushes, and then he heard a sniffing-snuffling noise, and pretty soon a voice cried:

"Oh, ha! Oh, hum! I smell fresh rabbit. Now, I will have a good supper!"

"That must be a savage bear or a fox!" cried the rabbit. "I guess this is the last of me!"

Then he saw two round circles shining in the darkness, two flashing, bright, shining things, and he was more frightened than ever.

"Oh, those are the glaring eyes of the fox or bear!" thought Uncle Wiggily. "I'm done for, sure!"

Then something made a jump for him, out of the bushes, but the rabbit crouched down, and the beast jumped over him. Then, would you ever believe it? those two shining things flew nearer, and instead of being the eyes of a fox or bear they were two, good, kind, lightning bugs, who were flitting about.

"Oh, you'll be a lantern for me, won't you?" cried the rabbit, anxiously. "Will you please light me out of these woods, and keep the savage beasts away?"

"Of course, we will!" cried the two lightning bugs. And they flew closer to the rabbit. Then the savage fox, for he it was who had made a jump for Uncle Wiggily, was so afraid of the sparkling lights, that he ran away and hid in the bushes, fearing he would be burned. Then the two bugs called for all of their friends to come and make the woods light so the old gentleman rabbit could see.

And pretty soon seventeen thousand, four hundred and eighty-three big lightning bugs, and a little baby one besides, came flying along, and the woods were almost as light as day, and Uncle Wiggily could see to hop on. The bugs flew ahead, shining themselves like fairy lanterns, and pretty soon the rabbit came to a nice hollow stump, where he remained all night. And some of the bugs stayed with him to keep the bears and foxes away.

Then, in the morning, after thanking the bugs, the rabbit traveled on again, and he had another adventure. What it was I'll tell you on the next page, when, in case my pussy cat goes in swimming and doesn't get her fur wet, the story will be about Uncle Wiggily and the Phoebe birds.

STORY XIX

UNCLE WIGGILY AND THE PHOEBE BIRDS

"Well, I don't seem to be finding my fortune very fast," said Uncle Wiggily to himself the next day, as he traveled on, after the lightning bugs had shown him the way out of the woods. "Here I've been tramping around the country for a considerable while, and all I've found was one cent, and that belonged to the chipmunk.

"I wish I could find a little money. Then I would buy some peanuts and sell them, and make more money, and pretty soon I would be rich, and I could go back home and see Sammie and Susie Littletail."

So he walked along, looking very carefully on the ground for money. All he found for some time were only old acorns, and, as he couldn't eat them, they were of no use to him.

"If Johnnie or Billie Bushytail were here now I would give them some," he said. But the squirrels were far away frisking about in the tops.

Now, as true as I'm telling you, a moment after that, just as Uncle Wiggily was going past a big stone, he saw something bright and shining in the leaves.

"Oh, good luck!" he cried. "I've found ten cents, and that will buy two bags of peanuts. Now I'll get rich!"

Howard R. Garis

So he picked up the shining thing, and oh! how disappointed he was, for it was only a round piece of tin, such as they make penny whistles of.

"Oh, dear!" cried Uncle Wiggily. "Fooled again! Well, all I can do is to keep on."

He went on a little farther, until he came to a place where there were a whole lot of prickly briar bushes, with red berries growing on them.

"Oh, ho!" exclaimed the rabbit. "Some of those berries will do for my dinner, as I'm getting hungry. I'll pick a few."

He was just going to pick some of the berries, when he happened to notice a big, red thing, like a red flannel bag, standing wide open near a hole in the bushes. And in front of the red place was a sign, which said:

"Come in, one and all. Everybody welcome."

"It looks very nice in there," thought the rabbit. "Perhaps it is the opening of a circus tent. I'm going in, for I haven't seen a show in some time. And, maybe, my friend, the elephant, will be in there."

Uncle Wiggily was just going to hop into the funny red opening that had the sign on it, when a little ant came crawling along, carrying a small loaf of bread.

"Hello, Uncle Wiggily," said the ant. "Where are you going?"

"I am going inside this red circus tent," said the rabbit. "Won't you come in with me? I'll buy you a ticket."

"Oh, never go in there - don't you do it!" cried the ant, and she got so excited that she nearly dropped her loaf of bread. "That is not a circus tent; it is only the skillery-scalery-tailery alligator, and he has opened his mouth wide hoping some one will come in, so he can have a meal. Don't go in."

"I won't," said Uncle Wiggily, quickly as he hopped away, and then he took up a stone and tossed it into the red mouth of the scalery-tailery-wailery alligator. The alligator shut his jaws very quickly, thinking he had something good to eat, but he only bit on the stone, and he was so angry that he lashed out with his tail and nearly knocked over a hickory-nut tree.

Then the ant crawled home, and Uncle Wiggily hopped on out of danger and the alligator opened his mouth again, hoping some foolish animal would walk into the trap he had all ready for them.

Well, in a little while after that, as the old gentleman rabbit was going along under the big tree, all of a sudden he heard a voice calling, rather sadly and sweetly:

"Phoebe! Phoebe!"

"My goodness, that must be some little lost girl named Phoebe, and her sister is calling for her," he thought. "I wonder if I could help find her?" For, you know, Uncle Wiggily was just as kind as he could be, and always wanting to help some one.

Then he heard the voice again:

"Phoebe! Phoebe!"

"Where are you?" asked the rabbit. "I'll help you hunt for your sister Phoebe. Where are you, little girl?"

But the voice only called again:

"Phoebe! Phoebe!"

"I guess she can't hear me," said the rabbit. "I'll shout more loudly."

Howard R. Garis

So he cried out at the top of his voice:

"I'll help you find Phoebe. Tell me where you are, and we'll go off together to hunt for her."

But this time the calling voice was farther off, though still the rabbit could hear it saying:

"Phoebe! Phoebe!"

"My goodness me, sakes alive, and a bottle of stove polish! I can't make this out," said Uncle Wiggily. "That little girl is so worried about her lost sister that she doesn't pay any attention to me. But I'll help her just the same."

So he hopped on toward where he heard the voice calling, and pretty soon, believe me, he heard two voices. One cried out:

"Phoebe! Phoebe!"

And the other one called just the same, only a little more slowly, like this:

"Phoe-be! Phoe-be!"

"Now, there are two of her sisters calling for the lost one," said the rabbit. "They must be very much worried about Phoebe. Perhaps a bear has eaten her. That would be dreadful! I must help them!"

So he hopped on through the woods, faster than ever, crying out:

"I'm coming! I'm coming! Old Uncle Wiggily is going to help you find Phoebe."

And then, would you believe me, Uncle Wiggily heard seven voices, all calling at once:

"Phoebe! Phoebe! Phoebe! Phoebe! Phoebe! Phoebe! Phoebe!"

"Oh, now the whole family is after that lost child," said the rabbit. "I had better go for a policeman." And then he happened to look up, and he saw a whole lot of little birds sitting on a tree, and each one was calling:

"Phoebe!" just like that. Really I'm not fooling a bit; honestly.

"Oh my! How surprised I am!" cried the rabbit. "Was that you birds calling for the little lost girl?"

"It was," said the largest bird, "but there isn't any lost girl. You see we are Phoebe birds, and that is the way we always sing. We always say 'Phoebe - Phoebe' over and over again. We didn't mean to fool you. It's only our way of calling."

"Oh, that's all right," said the rabbit. "I don't mind. It was good exercise for me to run after you."

Well, those birds liked Uncle Wiggily so much that they sang their prettiest for him, and asked him to stay to dinner, which he did. And he had chocolate cake with candied carrots on top.

And that's all to this story, if you please, but in case a red bird brings me some green flower seeds to plant in my garden so I can grow some lollypops, I'll tell you next about Uncle Wiggily and the milkman.

Howard R. Garis

STORY XX

UNCLE WIGGILY AND THE MILKMAN

Well, now I guess we're all ready for the story of the chicken who tried to roll an egg up hill, and it fell down, and was broken into forty-'leven pieces and the monkey - Oh dear! Did you ever hear of such a thing? I guess I must have turned over two pages in the story book instead of one, for to-night I'm going to tell you about Uncle Wiggily and the milkman, and not about the chicken and the egg at all. That comes in later.

Let's see then, we left the old gentleman rabbit just after he had met the Phoebe birds, didn't we? Well, a few days after that, as Uncle Wiggily was hopping along with the elephant, who had come back to him again, now and then, when he was tired, taking a ride on the back of the big fellow, all of a sudden they heard a voice crying:

"Ah, ha! Now I have you!"

"My! What's that?" asked the old gentleman rabbit.

"It must be somebody after us," answered the elephant. "But don't you be afraid, Uncle Wiggily, I'll take care of you, and not let them hurt you. Just get behind me."

So the rabbit got behind the big elephant, and, would you believe it? you couldn't see Uncle Wiggily at all, not even if you were to put on the strongest kind of spectacles, such as

Grandma wears. For he was hidden behind the elephant.

Then, in another moment a man with a long rope came bursting through the bushes, and he ran straight toward the elephant.

"Now I have you!" cried the man again. "You must come right back to the circus with me."

"Oh, it's you they want, and not me," remarked Uncle Wiggily, and then he wasn't afraid any more, and felt better, for he knew that he could still travel on and seek his fortune.

"Yes, they're after me," said the elephant sadly. "I guess I'll have to leave you, Uncle Wiggily. Do you want me to go with you, Mr. Man?"

"Yes, we want you back in the circus show."

"Will I have all the peanuts I want?" asked the elephant.

"Oh, yes," promised the man, "you may have a bushel and a pint every day, besides a pailful of pink lemonade."

"Then I'll come," said the elephant, "though I would like to have Uncle Wiggily come also. But he still has his fortune to find. Come and see me some time," he called to the rabbit.

"I will," said Uncle Wiggily. Then the man tied a rope around the elephant's trunk and led him away, and the big fellow waved and flapped his ears at the rabbit to say good-by.

"Now I must travel all alone once more," said Uncle Wiggily to himself, as he hopped on through the woods. "And I do hope I find part of my fortune to-day, even if it's only ten cents' worth."

Well, he was passing across a nice green field a little while after that when, all of a sudden, he heard some voices talking. He

Howard R. Garis

looked all around, but he couldn't see any one, and he wondered if perhaps there were fairies about. Then he heard a voice say:

"Now, children, hop just as I do. Take a long breath and then hop, and be very careful where you go."

Then Uncle Wiggily looked down in the grass, and he saw a mamma hoptoad and a whole lot of her little toads hopping along. The mamma toad was giving the little ones their morning lesson. And I just wish you could have seen how nicely those tiny toads could hop. One little chap, named Sylvester, hopped over a big stone, and his little sister, named Clarabella, leaped over a stick with a nail in it and didn't get hurt a bit.

"Ha! That is very good hopping! Very fine, indeed!" cried Uncle Wiggily, waving his ears back and forth. "I could hardly do better myself."

"Oh, it's very kind of you to say so," said the mamma toad. "Now, children, give a big hop for Uncle Wiggily."

Well, they all took long breaths, and they were just going to hop when the old gentleman rabbit suddenly called:

"Look out! Hold on! Don't jump!"

They all stopped quickly, and the mamma toad wanted to know what was the matter.

"Why, there is a big cow walking along," said the rabbit, for he could see over the top of the grass better than could the toads, and could watch the big cow coming. "If that cow stepped on you, why, you would never hop again," said the rabbit, and then he led the toads out of danger.

"Oh, I'm ever so much obliged to you," said the mamma toad to the rabbit. "You saved our lives."

Then she had all the little toads thank the old gentleman rabbit, and the mamma toad asked him to come to her house for dinner. Uncle Wiggily went, but the toad's house was so small that he couldn't get in, until he had made it bigger by scratching away some of the dirt around the front door.

Then he had a very good dinner, and he stayed all night at the toad family's house and watched the little ones hop some more, and he and the papa toad talked about the weather.

Well, in the morning when Uncle Wiggily got up and washed his face and paws, and combed out his whiskers, he suddenly heard all the little toads crying.

"Hum! Suz! Dud!" he exclaimed, "some of them must have the toothache." So he went down stairs, and there all the toad family were sitting around the breakfast table, but they weren't eating.

"What's the matter?" asked Uncle Wiggily, sadly-like.

"Why," said the papa toad, "the milkman hasn't come, and the children have no milk for their oatmeal, and I have none for my coffee, and I'm in a hurry to get down to the store where I work."

"That's too bad," said the rabbit. "Can't you use condensed milk?"

"We haven't any," spoke the mamma toad.

"Well, I'll hop out and see if I can see the milkman coming," said the rabbit, "for I can see a long distance." So he went out and he hopped up and down the street, and he looked up and down, but no milkman could he see. And the little toads were getting hungrier and hungrier every minute and they cried a lot, yes, indeed!

"This is too bad!" said Uncle Wiggily. "I guess that milkman

Howard R. Garis

must be lost. What can I do? Ah, I have it!" and away he hopped off toward the green fields. Pretty soon he came to where the cow, who had nearly walked on the toads, was eating grass, and, stepping up to her, Uncle Wiggily politely asked:

"Will you please give me some milk for the toads?"

"To be sure I will," said the cow, kindly, "and I'm sorry I nearly stepped on them yesterday." So she gave Uncle Wiggily a canful of fresh milk, for the rabbit had brought the milk can out with him. Then Uncle Wiggily hopped to the toadhouse as fast as he could, and the little toads had milk for their breakfast, and didn't cry any more.

Then, after a while, the milkman (who was a big puppy dog) came along and said he was sorry he was late, but he couldn't help it, because he had stepped on a thorn and had a lame foot and couldn't go fast, so they forgave him.

"Well, I'll travel along now, I guess," said Uncle Wiggily, and once more he started off to seek his fortune. And if you don't let your bathing suit fall into the water and get all wet, I'll tell you next about Uncle Wiggily's swimming lesson.

STORY XXI

UNCLE WIGGILY'S SWIMMING LESSON

Uncle Wiggily was so tired and worn out after running for milk for the toad family that he couldn't travel very far that day to seek his fortune. He slept that night in a doghouse, where a kind puppy named Towser lived, and Towser covered the old gentleman rabbit up with leaves and straw and kept watch so that no one would hurt him.

"For I have heard about you from Percival, the old circus dog," said Towser, the next morning when the rabbit awakened, "and I feel quite like a friend to you. Will you gnaw one of my juicy bones?"

"No, thank you," said Uncle Wiggily, "but if I had a bit of carrot I would be very glad."

"Don't say another word!" cried Towser. "I will have it for you in less than two shakes of a crooked stick, or a straight one, either."

So he ran out into the vegetable garden, and, very carefully he dug up a fine yellow carrot, which Uncle Wiggily ate for his breakfast. Then the rabbit rested all that day, and stayed another night with Towser. And Towser invited some of his friends over to call on the rabbit, and they had quite an evening's entertainment.

Howard R. Garis

Towser sang a funny song and stood on his tail, and Uncle Wiggily jumped over two chairs and a footstool, and a dog named Rover stood up on his hind legs and begged, and made believe he was a soldier with a broom for a gun, and did lots of tricks like that.

Well, the next day Uncle Wiggily felt well enough to go on with his travels again and so he started off.

"I will go part of the way with you," said Towser, "to see that no harm comes to you."

"Thank you, very much," said the rabbit, and so they set off together, the puppy dog carrying Uncle Wiggily's valise for him.

Pretty soon, not so very long, they came to a pond of water, and as soon as Towser saw it, he cried out:

"Oh, it is such a hot day I think I'll jump in and have a swim. Come on, Uncle Wiggily, have a swim with me."

"Oh, no, I can't swim," said the old gentleman rabbit.

"What! You can't swim?" cried the dog. "Well, every one ought to swim, for when they go on their vacation if they fall in the water they won't drown if they know how to keep themselves up. Watch me and see how easy it is."

So Towser set the satchel down on the bank and, taking off some of his clothes, into the water he jumped with a big splashy dive. Right down under the water he disappeared.

"Oh, he'll be drowned, sure!" cried Uncle Wiggily, who was much frightened. But, no. In a second up came Towser, shaking the water from his hair and eyes, and then he began swimming around as easily as a chicken can pick up corn.

"Come on in, Uncle Wiggily," he called. "The water is fine."

"Oh, I'm afraid!" said the rabbit.

"Then the first thing to do is to get so you are not afraid of the water," said the dog. "You needn't be. Just see; it will hold you up easily if you go at it right. Just keep your nose out, and don't splutter and splash too much and you can swim. Come in and I will give you a lesson."

So Uncle Wiggily got in the water. At first it took his breath away, but after a bit he got used to it, and he found that he could wade away far out. Then he tried holding his breath and ducking his head away under, and he found that he could do that and not be harmed in the least, and at last he got so he wasn't afraid at all in the water.

"Now for a lesson," said the puppy dog. "You must wade out so that the water is up to your neck, and then you face toward shore, so you won't be frightened. Then you just lean forward, gently and easily, and you kick out with your legs like a frog, and you wave your hands around from in front of you to your sides, and keep on doing that and you'll swim."

"I'll try it," said the rabbit.

So he tried it, but, all of a sudden, he cried out:

"Ouch! Oh, my! Oh, dear me! Oh, hum, suz dud!"

"What's the matter," asked the dog, looking around.

"A fish bit my toe," exclaimed the rabbit.

"Oh, I guess you only hit it on a stone," said Towser. "Fish are too frightened to bite any one. Come on, strike out and swim as I do."

Then Uncle Wiggily wasn't afraid, and soon he was swimming as nicely as could be. For you know to swim you must first not be a bit afraid of the water, for it can't hurt you. If ever you fall

Howard R. Garis

in, don't breathe - just hold your breath as long as you can. Then, pretty soon you'll come up, and if some one doesn't grab you, and you go under again, hold your breath until you come up once more and then some one will surely grab you.

"You must never breathe under water - just hold your breath," said Towser to Uncle Wiggily, and the rabbit did it that way, and soon he could even swim under water.

"Well, I'm much obliged to you," he said to Towser, "but now I must be on my way to seek my fortune."

So he said good-by to Towser and hopped on. And he hadn't gone very far before a big bear saw him and chased after him.

"Oh, I'll catch you!" cried the bear to the rabbit. Well, I just wish you could have seen Uncle Wiggily run! He ran until he came to a big river, and the bear was right after him.

"Now I have you!" cried the bear. "You can't get across the river."

"Oh, can't I?" asked the rabbit. "Just you watch and see!"

So Uncle Wiggily threw his crutch and valise across the stream, and then into it he jumped, and he swam just as Towser had taught him and he got safely on the other side and so saved his life, for the bear couldn't swim and Uncle Wiggily could. So you see it's a good thing to know how to swim, and I hope all of you, who are big enough, know how to keep up in the water.

Well, Uncle Wiggily got across to the other shore, and he looked back and there that bear was raging and tearing around as mad as mad could be, because the rabbit had gotten away from him. But I'm glad of it; aren't you?

Now I have another story for you, and, in case my typewriter doesn't fall in the lake and the fishes don't eat up the hair ribbon on it, I'll tell you about Uncle Wiggily in the bear's den.

Howard R. Garis

STORY XXII

UNCLE WIGGILY IN THE BEAR'S DEN

Well, here we are again, all ready for a story, I suppose, and I hope you had a nice time at the surprise party. Let me see now, what shall I tell you about? How would you like to hear about the old gentleman rabbit and the toadstool?

Oh, my! I just happened to remember that I promised to write about Uncle Wiggily getting into the bear's den, so of course I'll have to tell about that first, and afterward I'll write the story about the toadstool. I'll tell you this much, however, the toadstool story is very curious, if I do say so myself.

Anyhow, Uncle Wiggily was hopping along one fine morning, following a stormy night, and he was thinking about the swimming lesson he had had a few days before.

"I wonder if I have forgotten how to move my legs, and go skimming through the water?" he said to himself as he set down his valise, and leaned his crutch against a prickly briar bush. "I must practice a little."

And the old gentleman rabbit did practice then and there, going through all the motions of swimming, only he was on dry land, of course. Next he twinkled his nose, like a star on a very hot night, when you drink iced lemonade to keep cool, and then Uncle Wiggily hopped forward once more.

He hadn't gone very far before he noticed a grasshopper moving along so swiftly that the old gentleman rabbit could hardly see the legs go flip-flap. My, but that grasshopper did hippity-hop!

"Hold on there, if you please!" called Uncle Wiggily. "What is your hurry. Are you late for school?"

"There is no school now," said the grasshopper, as he sat on a daisy flower, "but I am hopping along to get out of danger."

"Danger? What danger is there around here?" asked the rabbit. "Do you see a fox, or anything like that?"

"No, but don't you hear that dreadful noise?" asked the grasshopper. "Listen, and you will hear it. It scared me so that I went away as fast as I could."

So Uncle Wiggily listened, and sure enough he heard, away off in the woods, a voice shouting:

"Help! Help! Help! Oh, won't some one please help me, or I'll be killed!"

"There, did you hear it?" asked the grasshopper, as he shivered and got ready to flit away again, "he said he was going to kill us."

"Oh, no! Nonsense!" exclaimed Uncle Wiggily. "That is some poor animal caught in a trap, and he's afraid of being killed himself. I'm going to see who it is. Perhaps it is a friend of mine."

"Oh, no! Don't you go!" begged the grasshopper. "For it may be the alligator with the skillery-scalery-railery tail."

"Oh, preposterous!" cried Uncle Wiggily, who sometimes used big words when he was excited. "I'm not afraid. I'm going to help whoever it is, and, perhaps, in that way I may find my fortune."

So the grasshopper, who was very much frightened, flew on, and the rabbit hopped toward where he could hear the voice still calling for help.

And whom do you s'pose it was? Why, the second cousin to Grandfather Prickly Porcupine was caught fast in a trap, and he was calling for help as loudly as he could call.

"Oh, I'm so glad you came along," said the porcupine to Uncle Wiggily. "Please help me to get my leg out of this trap."

"Of course I will," said the rabbit, and with his crutch he pried open the trap, and set free the nice little second cousin to Grandfather Prickly Porcupine.

"Oh, how thankful I am to you," said the porcupine, as he limped away. "If ever I can do you a favor I will." And, would you believe it? the time was soon to come when that porcupine was to save Uncle Wiggily's life.

Well, the old gentleman rabbit hopped on, looking all over for his fortune, but he couldn't seem to find it anywhere until, all of a sudden, as he was walking along by some big stones, he saw something shining, and picking it up, he found he had a silver twenty-five-cent piece.

"Oh, my goodness me, sakes alive and a piece of cherry pie!" cried the rabbit. "I've found part of my fortune! I'll have good luck now, and perhaps I can find more."

So the rabbit looked all about in among the stones for other money. But he didn't find any, and pretty soon he came to a place where there was a hole down in between the big rocks.

"Perhaps there is more money down there," said the rabbit. "I'll take a look." He leaned over, and looked down, and then - Oh, how sorry I am that I have to tell it, but I do, all of a sudden Uncle Wiggily fell right down that black hole.

Right down into it he fell, and he landed at the bottom with such a bump that he nearly broke his spectacles. At first it was so dark that he couldn't make out anything, but in a little while he could see something big and black and shaggy coming toward him, and a grillery-growlery voice called out:

"Who's there? Who dares to come into my den?"

"It is only I," said the rabbit. "I'm Uncle Wiggily Longears, and I came in here by mistake. I was looking for my fortune."

"Ah, ha!" cried the bear, for the shaggy creature with the grillery-growlery voice was a bear. "Ah, ha! That is a different story. I am very glad you dropped in to see me, Mr. Longears. I was just wondering what I'd have for my dinner, and now I know - it is going to be rabbit stew, and you are going to be stewed," and the bear opened the dining-room shutters so he could see to eat the rabbit.

"Oh, how can you be so cruel to me?" asked Uncle Wiggily. "I only came in here by mistake. I found twenty-five cents, and I was looking for more."

"Found twenty-five cents, did you, eh?" cried the bear, savage-like. "Give it to me at once! I lost that, it's my money!"

And he took the twenty-five-cent piece right away from Uncle Wiggily. Then the bear was just going to eat up the nice old gentleman rabbit, and Uncle Wiggily didn't know how to get away, and he was feeling most dreadful, when, all of a sudden, a voice sharply cried:

"Here, you let my friend Uncle Wiggily alone," and then some one scrambled down through the top hole of the bear's den.

"Who are you?" asked the shaggy creature with the grillery-growlery voice, and the bear gnashed his teeth.

"I'm the second cousin to Grandfather Prickly Porcupine," was the answer, "and I'm going to save my rabbit friend."

And with that the porcupine took out a whole handful of his stickery-ickery quills, like toothpicks, and he stuck them right into the soft and tender nose of that bad bear. And the stickery-ickery quills so tickled the bear and hurt him that he nearly sneezed his head off, and tears came into his eyes.

"Now's our time! Come on, let's get away from here!" cried the porcupine to the rabbit, and up out of the bear's den they scrambled, and got safely away before the bear had finished his sneezing.

"Oh, you saved my life," said Uncle Wiggily to the prickly porcupine, "and I thank you very much." Then they traveled on together, and they had an adventure the next day.

What it was I'll tell you soon, when, in case the boys who go in swimming don't duck my typewriter under water and make it catch the measles, I'll tell you about Uncle Wiggily and the toadstool.

STORY XXIII

UNCLE WIGGILY AND THE TOADSTOOL

"Were you much frightened when you were in the bear's den?" asked the prickly porcupine as he and Uncle Wiggily went along the road next day. They had slept that night in a hole where an old fox used to live, but just then he was away on his summer vacation at Asbury Park, and so he wasn't home.

"Was I frightened?" repeated the old gentleman rabbit, as he looked to see if there was any mud on his crutch, "why I was so scared that my heart almost stopped beating. But I'm glad you happened to come along, and that you stuck your stickery-ickery quills into the bear's nose. It was very lucky that you chanced to come past the den."

"Oh, I did it on purpose," said the porcupine. "After you got me out of the trap, and I scurried away, I happened to think that you might go past the bear's house, so I hurried after you, and - well, I'm glad that I did."

"So am I," said the rabbit. "Will you have a bit of my carrot sandwich?"

"I don't mind if I do," said the porcupine, polite-like, so he and the rabbit traveler ate the carrot sandwiches as they walked along.

"Well, I don't believe I'm ever going to find my fortune," said

Howard R. Garis

Uncle Wiggily sadly. "I began to have hopes, when I picked up the twenty-five-cent piece, but now the bear has that and I have nothing. Oh, I certainly am very unlucky."

"Never mind," said the porcupine, "I'll help you look." But even with the sharp eyes, and the sharp, stickery-ickery quills of the hedgehog, Uncle Wiggily couldn't find his fortune.

But it is a good thing the old gentleman rabbit had company, for as they were walking along under some trees, all of a sudden a big snake hissed at them, like a coffee-pot boiling over. And then the snake uncoiled himself and tried to grab the rabbit by the ears.

"Here! That will never do!" cried the porcupine, and then and there, without even stopping to take off his necktie, that brave creature stuck twenty-seven and a half stickery-stockery-stackery quills into the snake, and then that snake was glad enough to crawl away. Oh, my, yes, and a basketful of soap bubbles besides!

Well, it wasn't long after that before it was dinner time, and the two friends sat down in a place where there were a lot of toadstools to eat their lunch. They sat on the low toadstools, and the higher ones they used for tables, each one having a toadstool table for himself, just like in a restaurant.

"Now, this is what I call real jolly," said the porcupine, as he ate his third piece of hickory-nut pie with carrot sauce on it.

"Yes, it is real nice," said the rabbit. "After all, it isn't so bad to go hunting for your fortune when you have company, but it's not so much fun all alone."

Well, the two friends were just finishing their meal, and they were getting ready to travel on, when, all at once, there was a terrible crashing sound in the bushes, just as if some one was breaking them all to pieces.

"My! What's that?" asked the porcupine, preparing to pull out some more of his stickery-ickery quills.

"It sounds like the elephant," said the rabbit, as he looked around for a safe place in which to hide in case it should happen to be the bear coming after him.

"Oh, if it's the elephant, we don't have to worry. He is a friend of ours," said the porcupine.

Well, the crashing in the bushes still kept up, and then before you could tickle your pussy cat under the chin-chopper, there burst out of the middle of a prickly briar bush a great big alligator - the same one who once before had tried to catch Uncle Wiggily.

"Oh, look!" cried the porcupine. "He's after us."

"Indeed, I am!" exclaimed the 'gator. "I'll have a fine meal in about a minute. I'll pull all your quills out, and eat you with strawberry sauce on; prickly porcupine."

"Oh, don't you let him do it!" cried Uncle Wiggily. "Stick some of your quills in him, and make him go away, Mr. Porcupine."

"It wouldn't do any good," said the porcupine. "You see, the alligator has such a thick skin on him that even a bullet will hardly go through, so my quills won't hurt him. I guess we had better run away."

Well, they started to run away, but the 'gator, with his skillery-scalery tail, chased after them, and he could go very quickly, too, let me tell you. Right after Uncle Wiggily and the porcupine the alligator raced, and he almost caught both of them. Then the porcupine saw a hole just big enough for him to squeeze down, but not big enough for the alligator to come after.

Howard R. Garis

Down into this hole jumped the prickly porcupine, and he was safe, but there was no hole for Uncle Wiggily to hide in, and the alligator was close after him.

"Jump up on a toadstool, and maybe he can't get you!" called the porcupine, sticking the end of his nose out of the hole.

"I will!" cried the rabbit, and up on top of the biggest toadstool he landed with a jump.

"Oh, I can easily get you off there!" yelled the alligator, savage-like. "I'll have you down in a minute."

He reached up with his claws to get the rabbit, and Uncle Wiggily got right in the middle of the toadstool, as far away as he could, but it wasn't very far. The alligator's claws almost had him, when all of a sudden that toadstool quickly began to grow up tall. Taller and taller it grew, for toadstools grow very fast you know. Higher and higher it went, like an elevator, taking Uncle Wiggily up with it.

"Oh, now I'm safe!" cried the rabbit, for he was quite high in the air by this time.

"No, you're not. I'll get you yet!" cried the alligator, as he reared up on the end of his skillery-scalery tail. He made a grab for the rabbit, but the kind toadstool at once grew itself up as tall as the church steeple, with Uncle Wiggily still on top, and then, of course, the alligator couldn't reach him.

"Oh, now I'm safe, but how ever am I going to get down?" thought the rabbit, for the alligator was still there. But, in another minute, along came a policeman dog, and with his club he made that alligator run away back to the swamp where he belonged. Then the toadstool began to get smaller and smaller, and it sank down close to the ground again and lowered the rabbit just like on an elevator in a store, and Uncle Wiggily was safe on earth once more. And he was very thankful to the toadstool, which grew up so quickly just in time.

"Well, we'd better get along once more," said Uncle Wiggily to the prickly porcupine, after he had thanked the dog-policeman. So the two friends set off together through the woods, and the next day something else happened to them.

I'll tell you what it was on the next page, when, in case the iceman brings me some hot chocolate to put on my bread and butter, the bedtime story will be about Uncle Wiggily and the chickie.

Howard R. Garis

STORY XXIV

UNCLE WIGGILY AND THE CHICKIE

"Well, what shall we do to-day?" asked the second cousin to Grandfather Prickly Porcupine, as he crawled out of his bed of dried leaves, and looked over to where Uncle Wiggily was washing his whiskers. "Are we going to travel some more?"

"Oh, yes," answered the old gentleman rabbit, "we must still keep on, for I have yet to find my fortune."

"What are you going to do with your fortune when you find it?" asked the porcupine. "Will you buy a million ice cream cones with the money?"

"Oh, my goodness sakes alive, and a pot of mustard, no!" replied Uncle Wiggily. "If I ate as many cones as that I would have indigestion, as well as rheumatism. When I find my fortune I am going back home, and I'll buy something for Sammie and Susie Littletail, and for Johnnie and Billie Bushy-tail, and for all my other animal friends, including Grandfather Goosey Gander. That's what I'll do when I find my fortune."

"Very good," said the porcupine, and then he got up and washed his face and paws. And he wiped them on the towel after the old gentleman rabbit, instead of before him, for you see when the porcupine soaked up the water off his face he left some of his stickery-stockery quills sticking in the towel, and if Uncle Wiggily had used it then he might have been scratched.

But, as it was, the rabbit didn't even get tickled, and very glad of it he was, too. Oh, my, yes, and some pepper hash in addition.

Well, Uncle Wiggily and the porcupine had their breakfast and then they started off. They hadn't gone very far before they met a locust sitting on the low limb of a tree. And this locust was buzzing his wings like an electric fan, and making more noise than you could shake your handkerchief at on a Tuesday morning.

"Why do you do that?" asked the rabbit.

"To keep myself cool," said the locust. "I am fanning myself with my buzzy wings for it is going to be a very hot day."

"Then we must keep in the shade as we travel along," said the porcupine, and that is what he and the old gentleman rabbit did. And it is a good thing they did so, for, as they walked along where it was cool and dark, beneath clumps of ferns, and under big, tall trees, they passed by a place where a bad snake lived.

"Look out! There's the snake's hole!" cried Uncle Wiggily, and he jumped to one side.

"Ha! I'm ready for him!" called the porcupine, and he got some of his stickery quills ready to jab into the snake. But the snake was out on a big rock, sunning himself in the hot sun, though when he heard the rabbit and porcupine talking he made a jump for them and tried to catch them.

But you see they were in the cool shadows, and the snake's eyes were blinded by the sun, so he could not see very well, and thus the rabbit and his friend escaped.

"I tell you it is a good thing we heard the locust sing, and that we kept in the shade, or else we might have stepped right on that snake and he'd have bitten and killed us," said the porcupine, and Uncle Wiggily said that this was true.

Well, they kept on and on, and pretty soon they sat down in the shade of a mulberry tree and ate their lunch. Then they rested a bit, and in the afternoon they traveled on farther.

And, just as they were passing by a large, gray rock, that had nice, green moss on it, all of a sudden they heard something calling like this:

"Cheep! Cheep! Chip-cheep-cheep! Oh, cheep! Peep! Peep!"

"What's that?" asked Uncle Wiggily in a whisper.

"I don't know. Maybe a burglar fox," answered the porcupine also, in a whisper. "But I'm all ready for him."

So he got out some of his sharpest stickery quills to jab into the burglar fox, and the noise still kept up:

"Cheep! Cheep! Yip! Yip! Yap! Yap! Cheep-chap!"

"That doesn't sound like a fox," said the rabbit, listening with his two ears.

"No, it doesn't," admitted the porcupine, and he stuck his quills back again like pins in a cushion. "Perhaps it is the skillery-scalery alligator, and my quills would be of no use against him," he went on.

Then, all at once, before Uncle Wiggily could make his nose twinkle like a star of a frosty night more than two times, there was a rustling in the bushes, and out popped a poor, little white chickie - only she wasn't so very white now, for her feathers were all wet and muddy.

"Cheep-chap! Yip-yap!" cried the little chickie.

"Why, what in the world are you doing away off here?" asked

Uncle Wiggily. "You poor little dear! Where is your mother?"

"Oh, me! Oh, my!" cried the little chickie. "I only wish I knew. I'm lost! I wandered away from my mamma, and my brothers, and sisters, and I'm lost in these woods. Oh chip! Oh chap! Oh yip! Oh yap!" Then she cried real hard and the tears washed some of the dirt off her white feathers.

"Don't cry," said Uncle Wiggily, kindly. "We'll help you find your mamma, won't we, Mr. Porcupine?"

"Of course we will," said the stickery-stockery creature. "You go one way, Uncle Wiggily, and I'll go the other, and the chickie can stay on this big rock until one of us comes back with her mamma."

"Yes, and here is a piece of cherry pie for you to eat while we are gone," said the rabbit, giving the lost chickie a nice piece of the pie.

So off the rabbit and the porcupine started to find the chickie's mamma. They looked everywhere for her, but the porcupine couldn't find the old lady hen, so he went back to the rock to wait there with the lost chickie so she wouldn't be lonesome. But Uncle Wiggily wouldn't stop looking. Pretty soon he heard something going "cluck-cluck" in the bushes, and he knew that it was the mamma hen. Then he went up to her and said:

"Oh, I know where your little lost chickie is."

Well, at first, that mamma hen didn't know who the rabbit was, and she ruffled up her feathers, and puffed them out, and let down her wings, and she was going to fly right at Uncle Wiggily, but she happened to see who he was just in time and she said:

"Oh, thank you ever so much, Uncle Wiggily. I was so worried that I was just going down to the police station to see if a policeman had found her. Now I won't have to go. Come along, children, little lost Clarabella is found. Uncle Wiggily found her."

So she clucked to all the other children, and the rabbit led them toward where Clarabella was sitting on the rock with the porcupine.

And on the way a big, ugly fox leaped out of the bushes and tried to eat up all the chickens, and Uncle Wiggily also. But the old mother hen just ruffled up her feathers and puffed herself all out big again, and she flew at that fox and picked him in the eyes, and he was glad enough to slink away through the bushes, taking his fuzzy tail with him.

Then the rabbit hopped on and took the mamma hen to her little lost chickie on the rock, and the rabbit and the porcupine had supper that night with the chicken family and slept in a big basket full of straw next door to the chicken coop.

Then they traveled on the next day and something else happened. What it was I'll tell you right soon, when, in case a little boy named Willie doesn't crawl up in my lap when I'm writing and pull my ears, as the conductor does the trolley car bell-rope, the story will be about Uncle Wiggily and the wasp.

STORY XXV

UNCLE WIGGILY AND THE WASP

"What would you like for breakfast this morning?" asked Mrs. Hen, as Uncle Wiggily and the porcupine got up out of their bed in the clean straw by the chickens' coop. This was the day after the rabbit found the little white chickie.

"Ha, hum! Let me see," exclaimed the rabbit, as he waved his whiskers around in the air to get all the straw seeds out of them: "what would I like? Why, I think some fried oranges with carrot gravy on them would be nice, don't you, Mr. Porcupine?"

"No," said the stickery-stockery creature. "I think I would like to have some bread with banana butter on and a glass of milk with vanilla flavoring."

"You may both have what you like, because you were so kind to my little lost Clarabella," said Mrs. Hen. Then she spoke to her children.

"Scurry around now, little ones, and get Uncle Wiggily and his friend the nice things for breakfast. Hurry now, for they will be wanting to travel on before the sun gets too hot," the mamma hen said.

So one little chickie got the oranges, and another chickie got the bananas, and still another chickery-chicken, with a spotted

Howard R. Garis

tail, got the carrots, and then Clarabella went to where Mrs. Cow lived, and got the milk for the prickly porcupine. Then Mrs. Hen cooked the breakfast, and very good it was, too, if I may be allowed to say so.

"Well, I guess we'll be getting along now," said Uncle Wiggily. "Are you still going to travel with me, Mr. Porcupine?"

"Oh, yes, I'll come with you for a couple days more, and then if you don't find your fortune I'll start out by myself, and perhaps I can find it for you."

So the two friends went on together. They traveled over hills and down dales, and once they met a lame rabbit, who had the epizootic very bad. Uncle Wiggily showed him how to make a crutch out of a cornstalk, just as Nurse Jane Fuzzy-Wuzzy, the muskrat, had done, and the lame rabbit made himself one and was much obliged.

Then, a little later they met a duck with only one good leg, and the other one was made of wood, and this duck wanted to get over a fence but she couldn't, on account of her wooden leg.

"Pray, how did you lose your leg?" asked Uncle Wiggily, as he and the porcupine kindly helped her over the rails.

"Oh, a bad rat bit it off," said the duck. "I was asleep in the pond one morning and before I knew it a rat swam up under water, and nipped off my leg."

"Oh, I'm so sorry," said the rabbit. "I'll tell Alice and Lulu and Jimmie Wibblewobble, my duck friends, to be careful of bad rats in their pond."

"That's a good idea," spoke the duck with the wooden leg, and then she said good-by and waddled away.

After that Uncle Wiggily and the porcupine traveled on some

more, and, as it got to be very warm they thought they would lie down in a shady place and take a little sleep.

Well, they picked out a nice place under a clump of ferns, that leaned over a little babbling brook, and touched the tips of their green leaves into the cool water. And, before he knew it, dear old Uncle Wiggily was fast, fast asleep, and he snored the least little bit, but please don't tell any one about it.

Then pretty soon the porcupine was asleep too, only he didn't snore any, though I'm not allowed to tell you why just now. I may later, however.

Well, in a little while, something is going to happen. In fact, it's now time for it to begin. Yes, here comes the stingery wasp. Listen, and you can hear him buzz.

"Buzz! Buzz! Bizzy-buzzy-buzzy!" went the stingery wasp, as he flew over the place where the rabbit and porcupine were sleeping. And the wasp flitted and flapped his bluish wings and lifted up the sharp end of his body where be carries his stingery-sting.

"Ah, ha! I see something to sting!" thought the wasp. "Now, I wonder which one I shall sting first? I think I will try the porcupine, and then I will sting the rabbit." Oh, but he was a bad wasp, though; wasn't he, eh?

Well, he was all ready to sting the porcupine, when suddenly the wasp heard a voice calling to him from the bushes.

"Don't sting the porcupine, Mr. Wasp, sting the rabbit," said the rasping voice.

"Why should I do that?" asked the wasp, as he looked to see if his sting needed sharpening.

"Oh, because if you sting the porcupine you might get stuck with his stickery-stockery quills," said the voice. "But the rabbit can't hurt you. Besides, if you sting him for me I will give you a popcorn ball."

"Why are you so anxious for me to sting the rabbit?" asked the wasp, as he flittered his steely-blue wings.

"Oh, if you do that it will scare him so that he won't know which way to run, and then, when he is all puzzled up, I can jump out on him and eat him up!" said the voice. "I have been wanting a rabbit dinner this long time," and with that out from the bushes crawled the bad fox.

"Very well," said the wasp, "I'll sting the rabbit on the end of his twinkling nose for you, and then you must give me a popcorn ball," for you know wasps like sweet things.

So the wasp got ready to sting poor Uncle Wiggily, and all this while the rabbit and the porcupine were peacefully sleeping there under the ferns, and they didn't know what was going to happen.

"Buzz! Buzz! Buzz!" went the wasp, as he flew closer to Uncle Wiggily. He was all ready to sting him, when a piece of bark happened to fall off a tree and hit the porcupine on his left ear, waking him up. He opened his eyes very quickly, thinking that a fairy was throwing snowballs at him, and then the porcupine heard the wasp buzzing, and he saw the wasp flying straight toward Uncle Wiggily to sting him, and next the porcupine saw the bad fox.

"Ha! So that is how things are, eh?" cried the porcupine, as he jumped up. "Well, I'll soon put a stop to that!"

So, before you could fan yourself with a feather, the porcupine took out one of his stickers, and he stuck the wasp with it so hard that the bad wasp was glad enough to fly away, taking his stinger with him.

"Now, it's your turn!" cried the porcupine to the fox, and with that he threw a whole lot of his sharp quills at the fox, and that bad creature ran away howling. And then Uncle Wiggily woke up and wanted to know what it was all about, and what made the buzzing and howling noises.

"You had a narrow escape," said the porcupine as he told the rabbit about the wasp and the fox.

"I guess I did," admitted Uncle Wiggily. "I'm much obliged to you. Now let's have supper."

So they ate their supper, and that's all I can tell you for the present, if you please. But, in case I see a little pig with a pink ribbon tied in his curly tail, I'll make the next bedtime story, about Uncle Wiggily and the bluebell.

STORY XXVI

UNCLE WIGGLY AND THE BLUEBELL

Well, I didn't see any little pig with a pink ribbon tied in his kinky, curly tail, but I'll tell you a story just the same if you'd like to hear it.

Once upon a time, a good many years ago, when - Oh, there I go again! I'm always making mistakes like that, of late. That's a story about a giant that I was thinking of, whereas I meant to tell you one about Uncle Wiggily, and what happened to him.

It was the day after the wasp had nearly stung him, and the old gentleman rabbit was traveling on alone, for the second cousin to Grandfather Prickly Porcupine had to go home, and so he couldn't help Uncle Wiggily hunt for his fortune any longer. ·

"Now take care of yourself," the porcupine had said to the rabbit, as they bade each other good-by, "and don't let any wasps sting you."

"What should I do, in case I happened to be stung?" asked Uncle Wiggily.

"Put some mud on the place," said the porcupine. "Mud is good for stings."

"I will," said the rabbit, and then he hopped on with his valise and his red-white-and-blue-striped-barber-pole crutch. Uncle

Wiggily hoped he would soon find his fortune, for he wanted to get back home and see Sammie and Susie Littletail, and all the other animal friends. So he looked around very carefully for any signs of gold. He also asked all the animals and flowers whom he met if they could tell him where his fortune was.

"No," said a warty-spotted toad, "I can't tell you, but I should think you would dig in the ground for gold."

So Uncle Wiggily dug in the dirt in many places, but no gold did he find.

"Perhaps you can tell me where my fortune is?" he said to a tailor-bird who was sewing some leaves together to make a nest.

"It might be up in the air," said the tailor-bird. "If I were you I should hop up into the air and look for it."

Well, Uncle Wiggily hopped up, but you know how it is with rabbits. They're not made to fly, and he couldn't stay up in the air long enough to do any good, so he couldn't find any gold that way.

"Oh, dear! I guess I'll never find my fortune," said the rabbit sadly-like. Then he saw a little blue flower, shaped just like a bell, hanging on a stem over a small babbling brook of water.

"Ah, there is a bluebell!" said the rabbit. "Perhaps she knows where my fortune is. I'll ask her, for flowers are very wise."

"No, I can't tell you where there is any gold," said the bluebell when Uncle Wiggily had asked her most politely. "All I do is to swing backward and forward here all day long, and I ring my bell and I am happy. I do not need gold."

"I wish I didn't have to have it, but I do. I need it to make my fortune, and then I can go home," said the rabbit.

"Very well," spoke the blue flower, as she rang her bell, oh so sweetly! so that it seemed to the rabbit as if she played a song about the blue skies, and birds singing and fountains spouting upward in the sun while pretty blossoms grew all around. "Go on, Uncle Wiggily, but if you don't find your fortune come back here, and I will sing you to sleep," she added.

"I will," spoke the rabbit, as he hopped away.

Well, pretty soon, not so very long, as he was walking on a path through the woods, Uncle Wiggily heard a voice speaking.

"I can tell you where to find your fortune," said the voice. "I know where there is a big pile of yellow stones, and I think they are gold. Follow me and I will show you."

"But who are you?" asked the rabbit, for he could see no one. "You may be the alligator for all I know."

"Oh, I'm not the alligator," was the answer. "I am a friend of yours, and I like you very much," and the unseen one smacked his lips. "But I can't come out and let you see me, for I dare not go out in the sun as I am afraid of getting too hot," the voice answered, "so I will just creep along through the bushes and I will wiggle my tail, and you can see it moving in the grass, and you can follow that without seeing me, and I will lead you to the pile of yellow stones."

"Very well," answered the rabbit, "though I would much rather see you. But go ahead and I'll follow, for I must find my fortune."

So the old gentleman rabbit saw the grass wiggling and he followed that, and he kept thinking of how rich he would soon be, and how many nice things he would buy for Sammie and Susie Littletail.

But if the rabbit had only known who it was he was following he wouldn't have been so happy, for it was a crawly snake, and that snake was only fooling Uncle Wiggily, and trying to get him off to his den so he could eat him. And that's why he didn't show himself. On and on the snake wiggled through the grass, shaking his tail, and the poor rabbit followed after him.

"Are we nearly to the gold?" asked Uncle Wiggily after a bit.

"Almost," answered the snake, making his voice soft and gentle.

The snake was nearly at his den now, and he was just going to turn around and squeeze the rabbit to death, when all at once a yellow bumblebee that was flying overhead looked down and saw the crawly creature, and the bee knew what the snake was going to do.

"Run away, Uncle Wiggily! Run!" called the bee, "the snake is fooling you!"

Well, Uncle Wiggily didn't wait a second. He jumped right over a briar bush and away he hopped as fast as he could hop, and the snake didn't get him, and, oh, how mad that snake was!

Uncle Wiggily hopped around and around in the woods and the first thing he knew he couldn't find the path, he was so excited. And the more he tried to find it the more he couldn't, until he sat down on a stump and said:

"I'm lost. I know I am! Lost in the dark, deep, dismal woods, and night coming on! Oh, what shall I do?"

Well, he was feeling very badly, and was quite frightened, and he didn't know what to do when, all at once he heard a bell ringing. Oh, such a sweet-toned silvery bell. "Ding-dong! Ding-dong!" it went, sounding very clearly through the woods. Then the bell seemed to say:

Howard R. Garis

"Come this way, Uncle Wiggily, come this way. Ding-dong!"

"Oh, that's the bluebell flower!" cried the rabbit. "How glad I am. Now I can follow the ringing sound and get to a nice place to stay for the night."

So he listened carefully, and the blue flower rang her tinkling bell louder than ever, and the rabbit could tell by the sound of it just which way to go, and pretty soon he was out of the woods and right beside the flower that was swinging to and fro in the wind, just like a bell in a church steeple.

"Oh, I'm go glad I could ring and tell you the way back here," said the bluebell. "Now lie down and sleep, and if there is any danger I will tinkle my bell and awaken you."

So Uncle Wiggily stretched out on some soft moss, and went to sleep. And there was some danger for him, as I shall tell you very soon, when, in case the rocking chair on the front porch doesn't go swimming in the molasses barrel, the next story will be about Uncle Wiggily and the Wibblewobble children.

STORY XXVII

UNCLE WIGGILY AND THE WIBBLEWOBBLES

Uncle Wiggily, the nice old gentleman rabbit, was sleeping on the soft moss under a clump of ferns, and over his head the bluebell flower was nodding in the night breeze, keeping watch for danger. For you remember, I dare say, that the flower had promised to awaken Uncle Wiggily in case any harm happened to come near him.

Hour after hour crept along, like a little mouse after a bit of cheese, and still the rabbit slumbered, and still the bluebell nodded her drowsy head, for she would not go to sleep while she was keeping watch.

"I think I will just take one little nap," said the flower to herself, after a bit, "just shut my eyes for a little while." So she did so, and then, all of a sudden, as quietly as a clock when it isn't ticking, there came creeping and crawling through the woods, the bad scalery-tailery alligator.

He was looking around sniffing, and snooping, and scuffing for something to eat, and pretty soon he sniffed and snuffed until he came to where Uncle Wiggily was fast asleep, dreaming that he had found his fortune. And the worst part of it was that the bluebell flower also was sleeping, and she couldn't tell the rabbit what was going to happen.

"Oh, I'll have a fine meal in about a minute," said the

Howard R. Garis

scalery-tailery alligator as he smacked his big jaws. Then he shuffled up closer to Uncle Wiggily, and was about to bite him when all of a sudden the nutmeg grater tail of the scalery alligator accidentally hit against the bluebell flower, and she awoke quickly.

"Tinkle! Tinkle! Tinkle! Ding-dong! Ding-dong!" rang out the bluebell, just like an alarm clock in the morning. "Ding-dong-dong! Tinkle! Tinkle!"

Up jumped Uncle Wiggily, rubbing the sleep out of his eyes. He looked through the woods, and by the light of the silvery moon he saw the grinning alligator, with his open mouth, close to him.

"Run, Uncle Wiggily! Run!" cried the bluebell, and then she made such a jingling-jangling noise that all the birds in the woods awakened, and by the moonlight, they flew down at that alligator, and stuck him with their sharp bills, so that he was glad to crawl away, and he didn't forget to take his scalery tail with him, either.

"My, that was a narrow escape!" said the rabbit. "I am glad he didn't eat me."

"So am I," said the bluebell, "and I'll not go to sleep again, either, I promise you."

So the flower stayed wide awake the rest of the night, and the rabbit slept on the soft moss, and in the morning he awakened and ate his breakfast out of his valise, and then, saying good-by to the flower and thanking her, he set off once more to seek his fortune.

Uncle Wiggily traveled on and on, looking in all the places he could think of for some gold, but he couldn't seem to find any. And then, just when he got on top of a little hill, and started down the other side he heard some one crying - no, I'm just a bit wrong, he heard three some ones crying - three separate and distinct cries.

"Oh, dear, I've got a sliver in my foot!" blubbered one voice.

"And I've stepped on a stone and there's a big bruise on my foot!" sniffled another voice.

"Oh! none of you is as badly off as I am," quivered a third voice, "for I've cut my two feet on a piece of glass! Oh, whatever shall we do?"

"My, I wonder who they can be?" thought the rabbit, for he could see no one as yet. "Maybe those are the little children of the burglar fox, and if they are, then the burglar fox must be somewhere around here, and I had better be careful of myself."

Well, the rabbit was about to turn, and run back down the hill, up which he had just come, when he saw something white fluttering like a piece of paper.

"A fox isn't white," Uncle Wiggily said to himself, "at least not the foxes around here. That must be something else." So he took another careful look, and he saw three nice little duck children - I guess you remember their names - Lulu and Alice and Jimmie Wibblewobble. And as soon as they saw the old gentleman rabbit, those three duck children exclaimed:

"Oh, joy! Oh, happiness!" and they didn't think about the slivers and the bruises and the cuts in their feet any more.

"My goodness me sakes alive and a potato pancake!" cried Uncle Wiggily. "What are you children doing so far away from home? You must be lost."

"We are lost," said Jimmie Wibblewobble, "all three of us."

"Yes," went on Lulu, "we are certainly lost, and it's Jimmie's fault, for he asked us to come."

Howard R. Garis

"Oh! it's not all Jimmie's fault," said Alice gently, as she looked at her brother. "You see, Uncle Wiggily, we are visiting our Aunt Lettie, the old lady goat, who lives in the country near here. We are at her house for our vacation, and to-day we started to go to the woods to have a good time, but we took the wrong path and we are lost, and I have a big sliver in my foot."

"Yes, and I stepped on a stone, and have a big bruise," whimpered Jimmie.

"And I've cut both feet on a piece of glass," cried Lulu Wibblewobble, "and Oh, we are all so miserable!"

"Well, well!" exclaimed the rabbit in a jolly voice, "this is too bad. I must see what I can do for you. First we will take the sliver out of Alice's foot," and he did so with a sharp needle. It hurt a little, but Alice never cried.

"Now for Jimmie's bruise," said the rabbit, and he took some soft green leaves, and made a plaster of them, and with some ribbon-grass for a string he tied the plaster on Jimmie's foot, and that was almost well. Then Uncle Wiggily made a little salve, from some gum out of a cherry tree, and bound up the glass cuts on Lulu's feet.

"Now, I will lead you to your Aunt Lettie's house," said the rabbit, "and you won't be lost any more." So the three Wibblewobble children felt much better and happier, and when they were almost at their aunt's house, a big hawk swooped down out of the sky and tried to bite Lulu. But Uncle Wiggily hit the bad bird with his barber-pole crutch, and the hawk flew away, flopping his wings and tail.

"Oh, how good, and brave, and strong you are!" cried Lulu to Uncle Wiggily, and then all three duck children kissed him. Soon they were at the goat-lady's home, and Aunt Lettie was very glad to see the rabbit gentleman, and also glad to have the children back. So she invited Uncle Wiggily to stay to supper, and very glad he was to do so.

He also stayed all night at Aunt Lettie's house, and he had quite an adventure, too, which I shall tell you about directly, when, in case the fire shovel doesn't slide down hill on a cake of ice and break its roller skates the next bedtime story will be about Uncle Wiggily and the berry bush.

Howard R. Garis

STORY XXVIII

UNCLE WIGGILY AND THE BERRY BUSH

"Well, children, I think I will soon have to be leaving you," said Uncle Wiggily Longears one morning to the three Wibblewobbles, when he had stayed all night at their Aunt Lettie's house. That was after the old gentleman rabbit had found the three ducks lost in the woods, you remember, and had taken them to where they were visiting the old lady goat. "I must pack my valise and travel on," said Uncle Wiggily.

"Oh, can't you stay a little longer?" asked Alice Wibblewobble, as she tied her sky-blue-pink hair ribbon in a flopsy-dub kind of a bow knot.

"Yes, do stay!" urged Jimmie as he tossed up his ball, which Lulu, his sister, caught. "We'll have some fun together and you can play on my ball team, Uncle Wiggily."

"Oh! I am much too old for that," said the rabbit, "though I like to watch you play. Besides, I have the rheumatism, and I have to keep on looking for my fortune. So I will travel forward once more."

"Well, if you must go, I suppose you must," said Aunt Lettie, the old lady goat. "But at least let me put you up a little lunch. Let me see, what shall it be? I think a tomato can sandwich, and some brown paper cake with paste frosting on would be nice. And then, too, I can give you some fine wooden pie."

"Oh, excuse me!" exclaimed the rabbit, "but while it is very kind of you, I cannot eat such things. I never could chew a tomato can, nor yet a wooden, or even a sawdust pie."

"No more you could," cried Aunt Lettie in confusion. "I was thinking of what I liked to eat. Very well, I will give you some carrots and cabbage and a piece of cherry pie. I know you will like those."

So she made Uncle Wiggily that kind of a lunch, and he put it in his valise, and after saying good-by to the old lady goat, and the three Wibblewobbles, off he started to seek his fortune once more.

On and on he traveled up some hills, and down others and through the woods, and pretty soon he came to a place where there was a big hole in the ground.

"Ah, ha!" exclaimed the rabbit, "perhaps this is a gold mine. I will get some gold dollars out of it and then I will be rich." So he went close to the hole and looked down it, but all of a sudden out popped a great big rat, and she gnashed her teeth at Uncle Wiggily and tried to bite him.

"What are you doing at my house?" she cried, real savagely. "Get away at once before I eat you."

"Indeed I will," said the rabbit, politely. "I thought your hole was a gold mine. Excuse me, I'll get right along," so he hopped away as fast as he could hop, very thankful that he had not gone down the hole.

Well, the next place he came to was where a great big stone was sticking out of the side of a hill. And the stone glittered in the sunshine just like diamonds or dewdrops.

"Oh, how delightful!" cried the rabbit. "This surely is a gold stone. I will break off some pieces of it and take them home, and then I will have my fortune."

　　　　　　　Howard R. Garis

So, taking his crutch, Uncle Wiggily tried to break off pieces of the glittering stone. But, my goodness me, sakes alive and a chocolate ice cream cone! that stone was very hard, and try as he did, Uncle Wiggily couldn't break off a piece even as big as baby's tiny pink toe.

"I'll just sing a little song, and then, perhaps, I can get some of the gold," he said. So he sang this song, which goes to the tune "Tiddily-um-tum-tum:"

"My fortune I've found,
On top of the ground,
I'm lucky as lucky can be.
But really this stone,
Is hard as a bone,
I wish that some one would help me."

After singing, Uncle Wiggily hammered away at the stone with his crutch again, but the song did no good. And then, all at once, before you could shake your finger at a pink pussy cat, out from behind the glittering stone there jumped the savage wushky-woshky, which is a very curious beast with two tails and three heads and only one crinkly leg, so that it has to go hippity-hop, or else fall down ker thump!

"What are you doing to my stone?" cried the wushky-woshky.

"Oh, excuse me," said Uncle Wiggily politely. "I didn't know it was your stone. I was only trying to break off a small piece for my fortune."

"Wow! Oh, wow!" cried the wushky-woshky, as savage as savage could be, and he gnashed the teeth in all three of his mouths, and he lashed his two tails on the ground. "I'm going to catch you!" he called to the rabbit.

"Not if I know it you won't catch me," said Uncle Wiggily bravely, and off he hopped down the hill.

"Yes, I will catch you!" cried the wushky-woshky, and off he hopped on his one crinkly leg after the rabbit. Faster and faster hopped Uncle Wiggily, but still faster and faster hopped the wushky-woshky.

"Oh, he'll surely catch me!" thought the rabbit. "I wonder what I can do? I know. I'll open my valise, and I'll scatter on the ground my nice lunch that Aunt Lettie put up for me, and the wushky-woshky will stop to eat the good things, and then I can get away."

So the rabbit did this. Out on the ground from the valise tumbled all the nice carrot and lettuce sandwiches. But the savage wushky-woshky gobbled them up with three mouthfuls, and didn't stop hopping after Uncle Wiggily on his one crinkly leg.

"Oh, he'll surely catch me now!" cried the rabbit.

"No, he won't! Jump up in the air, and come down inside of me!" cried a voice, and Uncle Wiggily saw a nice blackberry bush waving its long arms at him. "Jump down inside of me, where there are no thorns to scratch you," said the berry bush, "but if the wushky-woshky tries to come after you I'll scratch his six eyes out. I'll save you. Jump down inside me!"

"Thank you, I will," said the rabbit, and he gave a big spring and a hop, over the outer edge of the bush, and down he landed safely inside of it, not scratched a bit. Up came the three-headed, two-tailed and one crinkly-legged wushky-woshky, but when he saw the prickly briar berry bush he stopped short, for he did not want his six eyes scratched out.

"Come out of there!" cried the wushky-woshky to the rabbit.

"Indeed, I will not," said Uncle Wiggily, politely.

"Then I'll stay here forever and you can't ever come out," said the savage creature. "For if you come out I'll eat you!"

Howard R. Garis

"Don't let him scare you," said the briar berry bush to Uncle Wiggily, "I'll fix him," so the berry bush reached out a long arm all covered with stickers, and she stickered and prickered the wushky-woshky on his three heads and two tails and one leg, so that the savage creature ran away howling, and Uncle Wiggily was safe, and not hurt a bit, I'm glad to say.

So he stayed in the briar bush that night and had berries for breakfast, and the next day he had another adventure. What it was I will tell you on the page after this one, when the bedtime story will be about Uncle Wiggily and the camp fire - that is, if the cat across the street doesn't untie the pink ribbon off our pussy's neck and put it on his ice cream cone.

STORY XXIX

UNCLE WIGGILY AND THE CAMP FIRE

"Well, how do you find yourself this morning?" asked the berry bush of Uncle Wiggily as the old gentleman rabbit peeped out to see if the bad three-headed wushky-woshky had come back. "Are you all right?"

"Oh, yes, thank you kindly," spoke the rabbit, "but I was just wondering how I could get out of here to go on and seek my fortune without being scratched all to pieces."

"Can't you jump out just as you jumped in?" asked the bush, waving her prickly arms, but taking care not to so much as even tickle Uncle Wiggily.

"No, there isn't room enough for me to get started to jump out," replied the rabbit. "I'm afraid I'll have to stay here a long time, and I really ought to be going on."

"Oh, I have a plan!" suddenly cried the bush. "You are a very good digger, so why can't you dig a tunnel right under me? Start it inside here and curve it up so that it comes outside of my prickly branches, and then you won't be scratched."

"I'll do it!" cried Uncle Wiggily, so with his strong front feet he dug a tunnel, just as you sometimes make in the sand, and soon he was safely outside the berry bush.

Howard R. Garis

"Take some of my berries with you," said the bush, "so you won't get hungry."

"I will," answered the rabbit, and he filled his valise with nice, big blackberries. He felt a little sad about the nice lunch the wushky-woshky had eaten, but there was no help for it - that lunch was gone completely.

So Uncle Wiggily said good-by to the kind berry bush, and traveled on once more to seek his fortune.

"Watch out for the wushky-woshky," called the bush to the rabbit, as she waved her friendly stickery branches at him.

"I will," he said, and then he passed up over the hill and out of sight.

The first place he came to was an old hollow stump, where an old owl had once lived. The rabbit looked down inside the stump, but there was no fortune there.

The second place he came to was a curious little house built of bark, where an old dog, who was a friend to Peetie and Jackie Bow Wow, used to live, but the old dog was away on his vacation at Ocean Grove, so he wasn't at home.

"Perhaps there is a fortune in here," thought the rabbit, but there wasn't any and he went on.

Now the third place he came to was a little house, made out of clothespins, where a pussy cat lived, and the pussy wasn't home, for she had just gone to the store to get some milk.

But the rabbit didn't know this, so he went inside the house to see if there was any fortune there. And the first thing he saw on the mantelpiece was a tin bank, and when he shook it something inside of it rattled, and when he peeped in Uncle Wiggily saw a whole lot of pennies in the tin bank.

"Oh fine!" he cried, "now I have my fortune at last. Some one has gone away and left all this money, so I might as well take it."

Well, he was just putting the bank full of pennies into his valise, when the pussy came back with the bottle of milk.

"Oh! are you going to take my bank away from me?" she cried, very sadly. "I have been saving up my pennies for a long time, and now you have them."

"Oh, I wouldn't take them for the world!" cried the rabbit. "I didn't know they were yours, it's all a mistake," and he placed the bank right back on the mantel. "But perhaps you could tell me where to find my fortune," said Uncle Wiggily, and he told the pussy all about his travels.

"First we will have a drink of milk," said the pussy, and she poured out some for the rabbit. "Then I will go into the woods a little way with you and help you look for your fortune."

"Perhaps we had better take some lunch with us," said the rabbit, so he went to the store and got a nice lunch, which he put up in his valise, and then he and the pussy started off together to the woods.

They looked here and there and everywhere and even around corners, but no fortune could they find, and pretty soon it began to get a little dark. And then suddenly it got all dark.

"Oh, I can never find my way back home!" cried the pussy. "And I am afraid in these lonesome woods."

"Oh! don't be frightened," said Uncle Wiggily, who was very brave. "I will build a camp fire and we can stay here all night. I will cook some supper and in the morning I will take you home."

Then the pussy wasn't afraid any more. She helped the rabbit

Howard R. Garis

to gather up some dry leaves and little sticks, and also some big sticks, and soon Uncle Wiggily had a fine fire merrily blazing away in the woods, and it was nice and light. Then he took some leafy branches and made a little house for himself and the pussy and then they cooked supper, making some coffee in an old empty tomato can they found near a wrinkly-crinkly stump.

"Oh, this is real jolly!" cried the pussy, as she warmed her paws and her nose at the blaze. "It is much better than drinking milk out of a bottle."

"I think so myself," said the rabbit. "Now, if I could only find my fortune I would be happy. But, perhaps, I shall to-morrow."

Well, pretty soon Uncle Wiggily and the pussy became sleepy so they thought they would go to bed. They made their beds in the little green bower-house on some soft, dried leaves.

"And I must have plenty of wood to put on the camp fire," said the rabbit, "for in the night some bad animal might try to eat us, but when they see the blaze they will be afraid and run away."

So he gathered a big pile of wood, and then he and the pussy went to sleep. And in the middle of the night, as true as I'm telling you, yes, indeed, along came sneaking the wushky-woshky with his three heads and two tails and his one crinkly leg.

"Now, I'll have a fine meal," thought the wushky-woshky as he saw the rabbit and the pussy sleeping. "Which one shall I take first?"

But all of a sudden his foot slipped on a stone and he made a noise, and Uncle Wiggily awakened in an instant and cried out:

"Some one is after us!" Then the brave rabbit threw some wood on the camp fire, and it blazed up so quickly that it burned the whiskers of the wushky-woshky and he gave three howls, one with each of his mouths, and away he hopped on his one leg, taking his two tails with him.

"My!" cried the pussy, "it's a good thing we had the camp fire, or we would have been eaten up."

"Indeed it is," said the rabbit. "I'll keep it blazing all night." So he did this, and no more wushky-woshkys came to bother them. And in the morning the pussy and the rabbit traveled on together and they had quite an adventure.

What it was I'll relate to you almost immediately, when, in case a little girl named Elizabeth learns how to swim by standing on one toe and holding a red balloon under water, I'll tell you about Uncle Wiggily and the cowbird.

STORY XXX

UNCLE WIGGILY AND THE COWBIRD

"Do you think you can help me find my way back home again?" asked the pussy of Uncle Wiggily as they awakened the next morning, after having spent the night in the woods by the camp fire.

"Oh, I'm sure I can," answered the rabbit. "As soon as we have our breakfast we'll start off to look for your clothespin house."

Then Uncle Wiggily made up the camp fire again, putting on some more wood, and he boiled the coffee, in a tomato can, and fried some pieces of bacon he had in his valise. The way he cooked them was to take a sharp stick and put a piece of bacon on the end of it, and then he held the bacon up in front of the blaze, where it sizzled away, and got nice and curly and brown, and oh! how good it did smell, and so did the coffee! Oh! it's great to cook over a camp fire when the smoke doesn't get in your eyes and when it doesn't rain.

"Now we must put out the fire," said the rabbit, as he and the pussy were ready to go look for the clothespin house.

"Why must we do that, Uncle Wiggily?"

"Oh, so that it will not set fire to the woods, and burn down the nice trees after we are gone. Always put out your camp fire when you leave it," said the rabbit, as he threw water on the blaze, making clouds of steam.

Well, he and the pussy traveled on for some time longer together, but somehow or other they couldn't seem to find the place where the pussy lived, and the little cat was beginning to be sorry that she had gone camping in the woods.

"Oh, I know I'll never find my home again!" she cried.

"Oh, yes, we will," said the rabbit kindly. "Don't worry."

And just then they heard some one else crying, a little, tiny, sobbing voice.

"What's that?" exclaimed the pussy. "Perhaps it is one of the skillery-scalery alligator's children."

"No, I do not think so," said the rabbit. "It sounds to me as if some one else were lost in the woods, and I may have to find their home, too. We'll take a look."

So they looked all around, but they couldn't seem to find any one, though the crying was still to be heard.

"That's queer," said the rabbit, "I'll call to them."

So he called as loudly as he could like this:

"Is any one lost? Do you want me to help you find your home?"

"Oh, I'd be very glad to have you help me," said the crying voice, "but I am not lost."

"Then who are you, and what is the matter?" asked the rabbit.

"Oh, I am a robin bird," was the answer, "and I am in this bush over your heads."

Howard R. Garis

"Ha, no wonder we couldn't see you," said the rabbit, as he and the pussy looked up, and there, sure enough, was the nice mamma robin bird, and she was crying, as she sat in the bush.

"What is the matter?" asked the rabbit.

"I will tell you," said the robin. "You know there is a bird called the cowbird or cuckoo, and that bird is too lazy to build a nest for itself. So what do you think it does?"

"What?" asked the pussy.

"Why it goes around, laying its eggs in the nests of other birds," said the robin. "Then we birds have to hatch out the cowbird's eggs, and when her children come out they are so unpleasant that they shove our little birdies right out of the nest, and eat all the things we mamma birds bring home to our little ones."

"Ha! That is very unpleasant, to say the least," spoke the rabbit. "And are there any cowbirds in your nest now, Mrs. Robin?"

"Not yet, but there are three of the cowbird's eggs here, and they will soon hatch out."

"Why don't you toss out the cowbird's eggs?" asked the pussy. "Then you won't have to hatch them."

"I would," said the robin, "only I am not strong enough, for I have been ill, and my husband is out of work and he is looking for some. So I don't know what to do about it. Oh, dear!" and she cried again.

"Ha! We must see what we can do," said Uncle Wiggily, who always liked to help people who were in trouble. "I think I have a plan."

"What is it?" asked the robin.

"Well, I can't climb up that bush, for my paws are not built for that sort of thing, but the pussy can climb very nicely, as she has sharp claws."

"Indeed I can," said the pussy, "and I will, and I'll throw out the cowbird's eggs for you, so those bad birds won't bother your little birds."

So Uncle Wiggily gave the pussy a boost up the bush, in which the robin's nest was built, and then the pussy, with her sharp claws climbed up the rest of the distance all alone very nicely.

"Now show me which are the eggs of the cowbird?" said the kittie-cat to the robin when the nest was reached. So the robin mamma pointed out the eggs with her claw, and then with her foot the pussy clawed those cowbird eggs out on the ground where they wouldn't hatch.

"Now, that will be the last of those bad birds," said the pussy as she started to climb down to where Uncle Wiggily was waiting for her.

"Yes, indeed, and thank you very much," spoke the robin. "Now, my little ones will have a chance to grow and live."

And just then there was a fluttering and a rustling in the bushes, and the bad cowbird came flying past. And when she saw what had been done, and how her eggs had been tossed out of the robin's nest where they didn't belong, that cowbird flew at the pussy and was going to pick her eyes out.

But Uncle Wiggily took his crutch, and tickled the cowbird so that she sneezed, and had to fly away without doing any harm. And Uncle Wiggily called after her that she ought to be ashamed of herself not to build her own nests. And I guess that cowbird was ashamed, but I'm not sure. Anyhow she came back a little later and gathered up her eggs off the ground, and flew away with them, and what she did with them I'll tell you; oh, just as soon as you like.

Howard R. Garis

The bedtime story then will be about Uncle Wiggily and the tailor bird - that is, if the needle and thread don't dance up and down on the pin cushion, and make it full of holes so the sawdust stuffing comes out and tickles the baby's pink toes.

STORY XXXI

UNCLE WIGGILY AND THE TAILOR BIRD

After Uncle Wiggily and the pussy had helped the robin get the cowbird's eggs out of her nest, as I told you in the story before this, the rabbit and the kittie stayed in the woods a little while talking to the mamma bird.

"I should like to see the little robins hatch out of the eggs," said the pussy, as she frisked her tail about and smoothed out her fur.

"So should I," added Uncle Wiggily.

"I will gladly let you see my little birdies hatch," spoke the robin, "but it will take nearly a week yet, and you will have to wait."

"Oh, I can't wait as long as that," went on the rabbit. "I must be off to seek my fortune."

"Yes, and I must go and find my clothespin house," said the pussy.

So they said good-by to the mamma robin, and away the pussy and Uncle Wiggily went, over the hills and down the dales through the woods and over little brooks.

Pretty soon they came to a place in the woods where there

Howard R. Garis

were a whole lot of flowers nodding their heads in the wind, and it was such a pretty place that Uncle Wiggily and the pussy stayed there a little while. And in about a minute they heard something flying through the bushes and out flew that same cowbird, and she laughed just as hard as she could laugh, as she passed along.

"Somebody is going to be surprised!" cried the cowbird and she fluttered her wings at the rabbit and the kittie, and then she hid herself off in the woods.

"I wonder what she means?" asked the pussy.

"I'm sure I don't know," replied the rabbit. "But did you notice that she didn't have her eggs with her?"

"Sure enough!" exclaimed the pussy. "She must have left them in some other bird's nest."

"Well, we had better keep on, for it is getting late," spoke Uncle Wiggily, "and I want to find your clothespin house for you."

On they hurried through the trees, and pretty soon - Oh, I guess about as long as it takes you to eat a stick of peppermint candy - they suddenly came to the pussy's clothespin house.

"Oh, here's where I live!" she cried. "How glad I am to get back home!" She hurried in through the front door and no sooner was she inside than she cried out:

"Come here! Come here, quickly, Uncle Wiggily! Did you ever see such a sight in all your born days?"

"What is it?" asked the rabbit, as he hopped in, and he was half afraid that there might be a burglar fox hiding in the pussy's house.

But it wasn't anything like that. Instead the rabbit saw the pussy pointing to her bed, and there, right in the middle of the feather pillows, were some eggs.

"The cowbird's eggs!" cried the kittie. "That's what she meant when she said some one was going to be surprised. Indeed, I am the one who is surprised. She brought her eggs here, thinking I would hatch them out for her, but I'll not do it!"

So the pussy threw the eggs out of the window, on some soft straw, where they wouldn't be broken, and pretty soon that cowbird came back, as angry as a lion without any tail. And she grabbed up her eggs, and this time she took them to the monkey, who played five hand-organs at once. And the monkey was a good-natured sort of a chap, so he hatched out the cowbird's eggs for her, and soon he had a lot of little calfbirds, and when they grew up they gave him no end of trouble.

"Well, now you are safe home," said Uncle Wiggily to the pussy, "I will travel on."

"First, let me fill your valise with something to eat," said the kittie cat, and she did so, and then the rabbit hopped on. He looked all over for his fortune, but he couldn't find it, and pretty soon it got dark night and he went to sleep in a hollow stump.

"Surely, I will find my fortune to-day," thought Uncle Wiggily, as he arose the next morning, and combed out his whiskers. It was a bright, beautiful sunshiny morning, and everything was cheerful, and the birds were singing. But, in spite of all that, something happened to the rabbit.

He was just going past a berry bush, and he was reaching up to pick off some of the red raspberries, when all at once a sharp claw was thrust out from the bush and a grab was made for the rabbit.

"Now, I've got you!" cried a savage voice.

"No, you haven't!" exclaimed Uncle Wiggily, and he jumped back just as a savage wolf sprang out at him.

"Oh, don't worry, I'll get you yet!" went on the wolf and he made another spring. But the rabbit was ready for him and ran down the hill and the wolf ran after him, howling at the top of his grillery-growlery voice, for he was very hungry.

My! how Uncle Wiggily did run. And the wolf ran also, and he was catching up to the rabbit, and probably would have eaten him all up, but just then a kind bumble bee who knew Uncle Wiggily flew off a tree branch and stung that wolf on the end of his nose.

That wolf gave a howl, and made one more grab for Uncle Wiggily, but he only managed to catch hold of his coat tails in his teeth, and there the wolf held on.

"Let go of Uncle Wiggily!" buzzed the bee.

"No I won't!" cried the wolf, most impolite-like.

"Then I'll sting you again!" cried the bee, and she did so, and the rabbit gave a great pull, and he managed to pull himself away from the wolf. But, alas! Uncle Wiggily's nice red coat was all tattered and torn.

"Oh, whatever shall I do?" cried Uncle Wiggily as the wolf ran away down the hill and the rabbit looked at the torn and ripped coat. "I never can go on seeking my fortune with a torn coat."

"I am sorry," said the bee, "but I can not help you. But if you see the tailor bird she may mend your coat for you."

So the bee buzzed away and Uncle Wiggily went on looking for the tailor bird. This is a bird that makes a nest by sewing leaves together with grass for thread. And would you believe me, in a little while Uncle Wiggily saw the very bird he wanted.

She was making a nest with her bill for a needle and some dried grass for thread, and she was sewing the leaves together.

"Will you kindly mend my coat for me where the wolf tore it?" asked the rabbit politely.

"Indeed I will," said the tailor bird. So she took some long, strong pieces of grass for thread. Then she made her sharp bill go back and forth in the cloth of Uncle Wiggily's coat and soon it was all mended again as good as new. Then the rabbit thanked the bird and started off again to seek his fortune and you could hardly see where his coat was torn.

Then Uncle Wiggily was very thankful to the tailor bird, and he stayed at her house for some time, helping her sweep the sidewalk mornings, and bringing up coal, and all things like that. And the old gentleman had some more adventures.

But as I have already made this book quite long, I think I will have to save the rest of the stories for another one. I'll get it ready as soon as I can for you, and the name of it is going to be "Uncle Wiggily's Fortune."

Just think of that! He really does find his fortune in that book, though he has quite some trouble, let me tell you. But bless your hearts! Trouble is only another kind of fun!

So now we will say good-by to Uncle Wiggily for a time, and soon you may hear more about him. Good-by and good luck to all of you.

Howard R. Garis

ABOUT THE AUTHOR

Howard Roger Garis, (April 25, 1873(1873-04-25), Binghamton, New York–November 6, 1962, Amherst, Massachusetts) was an American author, best known for a series of books, published under his own name, that featured the character of Uncle Wiggily Longears, an engaging elderly rabbit. Garis and his wife were possibly the most prolific children's authors of the early 20th century.

Garis also wrote many books for the Stratemeyer Syndicate under various pseudonyms. As Victor Appleton, he wrote about the enterprising Tom Swift; as Laura Lee Hope, he is generally credited with writing volumes 4–28 and 41 of the Bobbsey Twins; as Clarence Young, the Motor Boys series; as Lester Chadwick, the Great Marvel series and books featuring Baseball Joe; and as Marion Davidson, a number of books including several featuring the Camp Fire Girls. By virtue of his accessible characters and engaging plots, Garis was the one of the most influential children's authors of his day. Many of his books, especially the Uncle Wiggily books, are still widely read.

Prior to writing for Stratemeyer, Garis and his spouse Lilian Garis both worked as reporters for the Newark Evening News. He did some work on the side for WNJR also in Newark. Their children also wrote for Stratemeyer.

OTHER BOOKS BY THIS AUTHOR

Curly and Floppy Twistytail

Daddy takes us to the Garden

Dick Hamiltons Airship

Lulu, Alice and Jimmie Wibble Wobble

Sammie and Susie Littletail

The Curlytops and Their Pets

The Curlytops at Uncle Franks Ranch

The Curlytops on Star Island

Uncle Wiggily's Adventures

Umboo, The Elephant

Howard R. Garis

Choose from Thousands of 1stWorldLibrary Classics By

A. M. Barnard
Ada Leverson
Adolphus William Ward
Aesop
Agatha Christie
Alexander Aaronsohn
Alexander Kielland
Alexandre Dumas
Alfred Gatty
Alfred Ollivant
Alice Duer Miller
Alice Turner Curtis
Alice Dunbar
Allen Chapman
Alleyne Ireland
Ambrose Bierce
Amelia E. Barr
Amory H. Bradford
Andrew Lang
Andrew McFarland Davis
Andy Adams
Angela Brazil
Anna Alice Chapin
Anna Sewell
Annie Besant
Annie Hamilton Donnell
Annie Payson Call
Annie Roe Carr
Annonaymous
Anton Chekhov
Archibald Lee Fletcher
Arnold Bennett
Arthur C. Benson
Arthur Conan Doyle
Arthur M. Winfield
Arthur Ransome
Arthur Schnitzler
Arthur Train
Atticus
B.H. Baden-Powell
B. M. Bower
B. C. Chatterjee
Baroness Emmuska Orczy
Baroness Orczy
Basil King
Bayard Taylor
Ben Macomber
Bertha Muzzy Bower
Bjornstjerne Bjornson

Booth Tarkington
Boyd Cable
Bram Stoker
C. Collodi
C. E. Orr
C. M. Ingleby
Carolyn Wells
Catherine Parr Traill
Charles A. Eastman
Charles Amory Beach
Charles Dickens
Charles Dudley Warner
Charles Farrar Browne
Charles Ives
Charles Kingsley
Charles Klein
Charles Hanson Towne
Charles Lathrop Pack
Charles Romyn Dake
Charles Whibley
Charles Willing Beale
Charlotte M. Braeme
Charlotte M. Yonge
Charlotte Perkins Stetson
Clair W. Hayes
Clarence Day Jr.
Clarence E. Mulford
Clemence Housman
Confucius
Coningsby Dawson
Cornelis DeWitt Wilcox
Cyril Burleigh
D. H. Lawrence
Daniel Defoe
David Garnett
Dinah Craik
Don Carlos Janes
Donald Keyhoe
Dorothy Kilner
Dougan Clark
Douglas Fairbanks
E. Nesbit
E. P. Roe
E. Phillips Oppenheim
E. S. Brooks
Earl Barnes
Edgar Rice Burroughs
Edith Van Dyne
Edith Wharton

Edward Everett Hale
Edward J. O'Biren
Edward S. Ellis
Edwin L. Arnold
Eleanor Atkins
Eleanor Hallowell Abbott
Eliot Gregory
Elizabeth Gaskell
Elizabeth McCracken
Elizabeth Von Arnim
Ellem Key
Emerson Hough
Emilie F. Carlen
Emily Bronte
Emily Dickinson
Enid Bagnold
Enilor Macartney Lane
Erasmus W. Jones
Ernie Howard Pie
Ethel May Dell
Ethel Turner
Ethel Watts Mumford
Eugene Sue
Eugenie Foa
Eugene Wood
Eustace Hale Ball
Evelyn Everett-green
Everard Cotes
F. H. Cheley
F. J. Cross
F. Marion Crawford
Fannie E. Newberry
Federick Austin Ogg
Ferdinand Ossendowski
Fergus Hume
Florence A. Kilpatrick
Fremont B. Deering
Francis Bacon
Francis Darwin
Frances Hodgson Burnett
Frances Parkinson Keyes
Frank Gee Patchin
Frank Harris
Frank Jewett Mather
Frank L. Packard
Frank V. Webster
Frederic Stewart Isham
Frederick Trevor Hill
Frederick Winslow Taylor

<table>
<tr><td>Friedrich Kerst</td><td>Hayden Carruth</td><td>James Branch Cabell</td></tr>
</table>

Friedrich Kerst	Hayden Carruth	James Branch Cabell
Friedrich Nietzsche	Helent Hunt Jackson	James DeMille
Fyodor Dostoyevsky	Helen Nicolay	James Joyce
G.A. Henty	Hendrik Conscience	James Lane Allen
G.K. Chesterton	Hendy David Thoreau	James Lane Allen
Gabrielle E. Jackson	Henri Barbusse	James Oliver Curwood
Garrett P. Serviss	Henrik Ibsen	James Oppenheim
Gaston Leroux	Henry Adams	James Otis
George A. Warren	Henry Ford	James R. Driscoll
George Ade	Henry Frost	Jane Abbott
Geroge Bernard Shaw	Henry James	Jane Austen
George Cary Eggleston	Henry Jones Ford	Jane L. Stewart
George Durston	Henry Seton Merriman	Janet Aldridge
George Ebers	Henry W Longfellow	Jens Peter Jacobsen
George Eliot	Herbert A. Giles	Jerome K. Jerome
George Gissing	Herbert Carter	Jessie Graham Flower
George MacDonald	Herbert N. Casson	John Buchan
George Meredith	Herman Hesse	John Burroughs
George Orwell	Hildegard G. Frey	John Cournos
George Sylvester Viereck	Homer	John F. Kennedy
George Tucker	Honore De Balzac	John Gay
George W. Cable	Horace B. Day	John Glasworthy
George Wharton James	Horace Walpole	John Habberton
Gertrude Atherton	Horatio Alger Jr.	John Joy Bell
Gordon Casserly	Howard Pyle	John Kendrick Bangs
Grace E. King	Howard R. Garis	John Milton
Grace Gallatin	Hugh Lofting	John Philip Sousa
Grace Greenwood	Hugh Walpole	John Taintor Foote
Grant Allen	Humphry Ward	Jonas Lauritz Idemil Lie
Guillermo A. Sherwell	Ian Maclaren	Jonathan Swift
Gulielma Zollinger	Inez Haynes Gillmore	Joseph A. Altsheler
Gustav Flaubert	Irving Bacheller	Joseph Carey
H. A. Cody	Isabel Cecilia Williams	Joseph Conrad
H. B. Irving	Isabel Hornibrook	Joseph E. Badger Jr
H.C. Bailey	Israel Abrahams	Joseph Hergesheimer
H. G. Wells	Ivan Turgenev	Joseph Jacobs
H. H. Munro	J.G.Austin	Jules Vernes
H. Irving Hancock	J. Henri Fabre	Julian Hawthrone
H. R. Naylor	J. M. Barrie	Julie A Lippmann
H. Rider Haggard	J. M. Walsh	Justin Huntly McCarthy
H. W. C. Davis	J. Macdonald Oxley	Kakuzo Okakura
Haldeman Julius	J. R. Miller	Karle Wilson Baker
Hall Caine	J. S. Fletcher	Kate Chopin
Hamilton Wright Mabie	J. S. Knowles	Kenneth Grahame
Hans Christian Andersen	J. Storer Clouston	Kenneth McGaffey
Harold Avery	J. W. Duffield	Kate Langley Bosher
Harold McGrath	Jack London	Kate Langley Bosher
Harriet Beecher Stowe	Jacob Abbott	Katherine Cecil Thurston
Harry Castlemon	James Allen	Katherine Stokes
Harry Coghill	James Andrews	L. A. Abbot
Harry Houidini	James Baldwin	L. T. Meade

L. Frank Baum
Latta Griswold
Laura Dent Crane
Laura Lee Hope
Laurence Housman
Lawrence Beasley
Leo Tolstoy
Leonid Andreyev
Lewis Carroll
Lewis Sperry Chafer
Lilian Bell
Lloyd Osbourne
Louis Hughes
Louis Joseph Vance
Louis Tracy
Louisa May Alcott
Lucy Fitch Perkins
Lucy Maud Montgomery
Luther Benson
Lydia Miller Middleton
Lyndon Orr
M. Corvus
M. H. Adams
Margaret E. Sangster
Margret Howth
Margaret Vandercook
Margaret W. Hungerford
Margret Penrose
Maria Edgeworth
Maria Thompson Daviess
Mariano Azuela
Marion Polk Angellotti
Mark Overton
Mark Twain
Mary Austin
Mary Catherine Crowley
Mary Cole
Mary Hastings Bradley
Mary Roberts Rinehart
Mary Rowlandson
M. Wollstonecraft Shelley
Maud Lindsay
Max Beerbohm
Myra Kelly
Nathaniel Hawthrone
Nicolo Machiavelli
O. F. Walton
Oscar Wilde

Owen Johnson
P.G. Wodehouse
Paul and Mabel Thorne
Paul G. Tomlinson
Paul Severing
Percy Brebner
Percy Keese Fitzhugh
Peter B. Kyne
Plato
Quincy Allen
R. Derby Holmes
R. L. Stevenson
R. S. Ball
Rabindranath Tagore
Rahul Alvares
Ralph Bonehill
Ralph Henry Barbour
Ralph Victor
Ralph Waldo Emmerson
Rene Descartes
Ray Cummings
Rex Beach
Rex E. Beach
Richard Harding Davis
Richard Jefferies
Richard Le Gallienne
Robert Barr
Robert Frost
Robert Gordon Anderson
Robert L. Drake
Robert Lansing
Robert Lynd
Robert Michael Ballantyne
Robert W. Chambers
Rosa Nouchette Carey
Rudyard Kipling
Saint Augustine
Samuel B. Allison
Samuel Hopkins Adams
Sarah Bernhardt
Sarah C. Hallowell
Selma Lagerlof
Sherwood Anderson
Sigmund Freud
Standish O'Grady
Stanley Weyman
Stella Benson
Stella M. Francis

Stephen Crane
Stewart Edward White
Stijn Streuvels
Swami Abhedananda
Swami Parmananda
T. S. Ackland
T. S. Arthur
The Princess Der Ling
Thomas A. Janvier
Thomas A Kempis
Thomas Anderton
Thomas Bailey Aldrich
Thomas Bulfinch
Thomas De Quincey
Thomas Dixon
Thomas H. Huxley
Thomas Hardy
Thomas More
Thornton W. Burgess
U. S. Grant
Upton Sinclair
Valentine Williams
Various Authors
Vaughan Kester
Victor Appleton
Victor G. Durham
Victoria Cross
Virginia Woolf
Wadsworth Camp
Walter Camp
Walter Scott
Washington Irving
Wilbur Lawton
Wilkie Collins
Willa Cather
Willard F. Baker
William Dean Howells
William le Queux
W. Makepeace Thackeray
William W. Walter
William Shakespeare
Winston Churchill
Yei Theodora Ozaki
Yogi Ramacharaka
Young E. Allison
Zane Grey